I Can See Clearly Now

...

A Memoir

**Margaret Marie Hailey Crudup
and Irene Hailey Harrington**

Foreword

. . .

We don't always understand what God is doing. But we do hold on to His promises and know He will make a way.

This book is about an infant, a little girl, a young woman, a wife and then, a mother, overcoming the struggles in her life—life's circle of happiness, sadness, hard times and good times. But through all her ups and downs, she never questioned God.

My dear cousin, Margaret. You have exemplified what it really means to hold on to God's unchanging hands. You were chosen by God to show the world what He can do. No mountain was too high for you. You climbed some of the highest peaks in your life, but it didn't stop you. You went down to some of the lowest of life's valleys and God brought you out.

I pray that this book will open the eyes of our family. When times get tough, open this book, and read how God can forgive and bless you, no matter what your circumstances are. When you can't see your way, and you are tempted to give up, turn to God's Word. In seasons of doubt, turn to God's Word. In seasons of forgiveness, turn to God's Word.

When you read this book, you will see that God's promises are like stars—the darker the night, the brighter they shine.

I pray that this book will open the eyes of our family members who are spiritually blind. *"Blessed are your eyes, because they see; and your ears, because they hear." (Matthew 13:16).*

— *Irene Hailey Harrington*

Chapter 1

. . .

1946

Among the students of the small graduating class at Anson County Training School, one of the students stood out from all the rest. Her name was Effie Louise Hailey. Her parents and her eight siblings lived on Maple Lane Street, near Coley Hill. Lexie and Hattie Mae raised their children to work and always be respectful to all adults.

The Coleys owned most of the property on that side of town and were willing to hire young Negro children to work in their homes. But this young girl wasn't going for it! She had a mind of her own and wanted to do better than working in some white woman's house and raising her children.

Effie was outspoken! She didn't bite

her tongue when it came to defending herself. During all 12 years of her schooling, she tried to make the highest scores on her tests and entered every social club the school offered. She was a popular student, and the staff and students loved her.

The time had come for her graduation rehearsal. She gathered her things and walked through the path that led to the school. Effie thought, "I want to get a job and save my money for college, but who's going to hire me in this small town? The only jobs around here, are in someone's house. I don't want to be a maid for these white people. I will be the only girl in my class working in a house and making chicken change for a living. I want to be somebody when I get grown. I'd rather pick cotton in the fields and make some real money!"

Effie was daydreaming about her future. She was a gifted piano player, and she played for the A.M.E Zion Church that stood on the hill in Wadesboro, North Carolina. They couldn't afford to pay her, so they gave her "pound gifts" for her family. On a good Sunday, she was given a pound of potatoes, a pound of flour, or a pound of sugar. The family was always grateful for whatever was given. Her parents believed that if you gave yourself to God, He would always make a way for you. They taught Effie to use her talents for the Lord. "I'm smart enough to go to any college I want to," she said to herself.

When she arrived at school, the principal saw her coming through the door and asked her to come into his office. Effie didn't know what to think! "The principal wants me to come to his office! I wonder what he wants with me," she thought, as she walked into the office and stood in front of his desk.

"Young lady, have a seat," he said. Effie looked back at the chair in the corner of the small room and sat down. Then, he opened a letter and began reading. The letter was from Livingstone College in Salisbury, North Carolina. "Effie, you have been accepted to attend this college. If you want to go, we the people in this community will help you and will make sure you have the funds to go. You don't have to give me an answer now. Go home and discuss this with your folks. You are amongst some of the smartest students to graduate from this school, this year. Oh yes! The class of 1946 will go down in history for Anson County Training School!" said the principal. Effie was speechless. She thanked her principal and headed to the gym for graduation rehearsal.

Later that day, Effie and her friends walked across Salisbury Street toward home. She was so excited about the meeting with the principal. "Girls, I have something to tell you," she said. The girls turned and looked at Effie, excited about learning a new secret. "What is it?" asked one of her friends. "I'm going away to school this fall!" she said. One of the girls grabbed Effie's arm and stopped her in her tracks asking, "What do you mean, you're going away to school?" Effie took the girl's hand and said, "I got accepted at Livingstone College in Salisbury. That's why I was late for rehearsal. The principal wanted to meet with me. He said my letter came to the school. I'm so excited, I could cry!" Her friends were excited for her. They talked about leaving Anson County to better themselves, too. "Will we see you before you leave, Effie?" one of the girls asked, with tears in her eyes. Effie gave all the girls a hug and reassured them that they would see each other again.

As the girls crossed the street, they went their separate ways. Effie walked quickly through the path to Maple Lane. She started running to get home before her father got home from work. When she opened the door, at her surprise, he was at the dining room table, sipping his afternoon coffee. "Hey, Daddy. Where is Momma?" she asked. Her father looked up and asked where she had been. "I'll tell you in a little bit. I am so excited I can bust!" she said, while hugging his shoulders. He looked at her and then he looked at his coffee. He poured some of the coffee and sipped it as he waited for her to tell him what was going on.

Her mother came through the kitchen door to the dining room and asked, "Did you go practice for graduation?" Effie nodded and sat in a chair. "Momma and Daddy, I have something to tell you. My principal received an acceptance letter for me to go to Livingstone College, in Salisbury, North Carolina. He wanted me to discuss it with you before I said yes. You know how much I want to go to college. Can I go, Daddy?" she asked.

Her father looked at her and said, "We don't have, ah, have any money to ah, send you up there. You got ah, to get you a job first! Miss Coley down the street's daughter ah, need somebody to, to, ah, clean up for her. Just five days a week, that's all ah, she needs. You go down there and make, ah, make that money!" he demanded. Her father may have stuttered, but it was clear to her exactly how he felt.

Effie didn't argue with her father and her mother didn't have anything to say about it. She just stood with her hands on her hips. There was silence in the whole house for a moment. Effie walked out with her head down and thought about what she would do. "Working for that woman!

Well, I guess I can give it a try. I'd rather pick cotton for a month or two. I think I can make more money that way!" she thought.

The next day, Effie's mother said that Miss Ann wanted to talk to her about a job. She put on one of her nicer dresses, combed her long, beautiful, black wavy hair and put on just a bit of lipstick before leaving.

On her way to Miss Ann's house, she saw one of her classmates, Edward. He was walking through Coley Hill to go play basketball with the neighborhood boys. "Hey, Effie! Hold up! Wait for a minute. Where're you going, girl?" he asked. "I'm going down the road to see about a job," she answered. He asked if she needed someone to walk with her, but she told him that she was okay.

"Effie, I want you to know, I think I'm in love with you, or something like that. I don't know even what love is, but I think about you all the time. You are so beautiful! Every time I see you, I just can't help it! I really want to see you again. Can I come by on Wednesday night?" Edward asked. Effie felt the same way, but she was too shy to tell him. She never had a real boyfriend before, just the boys who came to their house to visit with her brothers. They were too young and immature for her. "Yes! You can come over. I'll let my parents know that you will be coming to see me."

The two friends parted, and Effie reached her destination. She stepped onto the back porch and knocked on the door. A soft voice said, "Come in!" Effie opened the door and Miss Ann said, "Did you wipe your feet off? If you didn't, go back outside and clean your feet in the grass. I don't want anything on my floors. I keep my house clean!" Effie went outside and cleaned her shoes off on the grass, and said to herself, "I can't stand that ugly woman, and I don't want to work in her house! She thinks she's rich or something! My momma's house is cleaner than hers and her momma's!"

Effie walked back to the house and went inside the kitchen. Miss Ann showed her what she wanted done. She wanted Effie to work five days a week, seven hours each day. "Clean the kitchen, bathroom, and living room. Clean all the bedrooms and change the linens on Friday. Mop the kitchen and bathroom floors every day. Wash clothes on Wednesday mornings and hang them on the line. Iron the clothes before you leave on Wednesdays. I pay $2 per day, and pay day is on Friday evening at 6 p.m.," said Miss Ann. "Do you want the job, Effie?" She answered, "Yes!" Miss Ann continued, "I expect you to be here bright and early Monday morning. Uncle Lexie has been so good to us. That's why I'm hiring you! I don't let just anybody come in my house. Now when you leave, close and lock the door behind you!"

All the way home Effie thought about the way Miss Ann carried on about that old house. "Why did she call my daddy her uncle? He is not her uncle! Lord, I know I'm not supposed to hate people, but this is an exception to the rule! I hate the way she thinks! Putting on like she loves my daddy! That's her way of getting him to bow down to her, like she's a queen or something. Yes! I'm going to school and get my education! I want to live a better life than my poor Momma and Daddy. Lord, with your help and some more people around here too, I'm going to leave this one-horse town and make a decent living for myself!" she thought.

Graduation Day, 1946

The time and day were here. The Hailey family, and all the siblings except Lucius, Walter, Robert, and Fannie Mae were going. The boys were in the Army and Fannie Mae had moved to New York City to live with relatives. Effie's brothers and sister were dressed in their Sunday attire. Her mother always looked her best whenever there was a special occasion. Lexie wore the special suit and hat he purchased from Curry & Andrews Men's Clothing Store.

This family was proud of their daughter. She had accomplished a lot in her teenage years. She was a Crawford girl!

The Crawford sisters and brothers were well known in Anson County. All the families in the community knew them. The Hailey side of her family were known to be somebody whenever you spoke of one of them!

Effie's uncle, Alexander, was a very prestigious man in the town of Wadesboro. He was a chef and waiter for some of the rich and famous in the county. Effie was well known in the community too. She played the piano for the big Methodist church that sat on the hill off Salisbury Street. She was a self-taught piano player. "A gift from God," everyone would say. The Methodist people were proud to have her as a member.

Graduation started at 9 a.m. The Class of 1946 was small, but many proud Negro family members attended the ceremony. The principal encouraged the graduates to never forget who was responsible for their success. He told them that God would carry them through all their storms in life. "Be thankful for where you are, because life will be better for you, your

children, and for the rest of the generations that will follow you," he said.

When the time came to give the diplomas, the entire Hailey family stood and shouted loudly for Effie Louise Hailey. God made the way for her to complete her high school education. She was proud of herself and appreciated the sacrifices that her parents made for her along the way.

Her mom prepared dinner for the family and other friends who attended the ceremony. Someone asked Effie to play a song and she didn't hesitate. She opened the piano and started playing, "How I Got Over," one of her favorite songs to play for a closing hymn at church.

Everyone sat in the living room with plates of food on their laps. The men in the house ate at the table with Lexie. They laughed and talked about the news and enjoyed all the food they wanted. The house was filled with love and laughter.

Later that evening, Effie heard a knock at the front door. It was Edward! One of the boys let him in. As he entered the living room, her father got up to see who he was. He walked over to the young man and asked, "Ain't you ah, one of the Elliott boys ah, ah, across the street?" Edward looked at Lexie and said, "Yes sir, I am!" Lexie knew his people and wanted to know why he was at his house. He looked at Edward and asked, "Who did you come to see?" Edward answered, "I'm here to talk with Effie!" Lexie looked at Edward and didn't like what he heard. He said, "Don't you stay too long, you hear me? It's getting late and we do our house and garden work on Saturday morning. When everybody leaves here, you better be going out that door too! Effie ain't grown, yet! She still in my house! You hear me? I mean every word I said!" Edward turned towards the front door and said, "Yes, sir! I understand."

Saturday Morning Chores

It was wash day. Everyone had chores to do. The boys cleaned their room, and the girls gathered the dirty clothes for wash-ing. Hattie moved the wash pot closer to the tin tubs. She put dry wood under the pot and lit it with a match. Then the boys filled the pot with water. "Don't forget to fill the tin tubs, too—one for washing and the other for rinsing. Don't leave this house until we finish these clothes," she said. The boys did as they were asked. Effie mopped the floors and cleaned the living room and kitchen. If you wanted a happy mother in the house, you had better clean the house like Hattie wanted it cleaned.

While everyone was busy cleaning the house and washing clothes, Lexie was getting ready to go to his lodge meeting. He dyed his hair black every Saturday. First, he would wash his white gloves and apron. Washing them by hand was the only way they would get snow white. Everything had to be perfect for his lodge brothers. "Ah, don't move my wash pan off the back porch!" he yelled to Hattie. She knew how he was. It didn't bother her when he yelled for something he wanted done. She just looked at him, and kept doing what she was doing.

The lodge meeting was over at 8 p.m.

Lexie walked with one of his lodge brothers who lived on his street. They had the same conversation every Saturday night. They loved to talk about the good old days, especially about when they were children. You could hear the two men laughing all the way down the street. When Lexie got near his house, he heard someone talking. Effie and Edward were sitting on the front porch. Lexie looked at Edward and asked, "What, what are you doing here? Didn't I tell you not to come unless I was here? You take, take me for a fool, don't you?" Edward got up and grabbed his hat, and said, "Yes sir, you did, but your wife said I could sit on the porch with Effie. I thought it was alright. We're not doing anything but swinging in the swing and talking." Suddenly, Hattie walked to the front door, and said, "Lexie, what is the matter with you? Leave those young people alone. Effie is a grown woman now. She will be leaving us soon. What are you going to do when she goes to college? You can't see who she's talking to then! I told Edward he could sit out here on the swing." Lexie walked inside. He went to his favorite chair and opened the newspaper. When Hattie came to the dining room, he looked at her and said, "You are a crazy woman!"

Effie came inside when Edward left. She saw that her father was still upset. She walked over to him and hugged his shoulders and said, "Daddy, I will be alright. You don't have to worry about me. I'm as grown as I will ever be. I have always done what you and Momma asked me to do. You got to pray for me now. Ask the Lord to be with me in everything I do. Trust God with my decisions in life. You have nine children. The boys are going away to fight in the war. The girls will leave home to be with other people of their choosing. Pray for us, Daddy, and don't scold us and our friends. I understand that you and Momma are facing some difficult times, now. We have always been here with you. You and Momma did the best you knew how in raising us. So, Daddy, don't be so mean to our friends. They have feelings, too! Are you still angry with me?" Effie asked. Lexie didn't say a word. He poured some coffee and sipped it until it was all gone.

. . .

Everyone was up at 8 a.m. getting ready for Sunday School. Lexie was the first one up, then Hattie. The girls got up and dressed while the boys were eating breakfast. "Mom, we are going, now," said Effie. The girls didn't have to walk far. They got to church by 9 a.m. Effie went to the adult class. She had graduated from high school, so she was considered to be an adult.

She heard the front door of the church open. When she looked back, it was her parents, coming to sit in their favorite seats. The Sunday school teacher took her place and said, "Good morning, class. We have an addition to our class this morning. Effie, we are glad to have you join the adult class." She continued to give the text for the class. "Would every-one open your bibles to Psalm 121:1-2." She began to read the scriptures: *"I look up to the mountains—does my help come from there? My help comes from the Lord, who made heaven and earth!"* Then, she asked the class a question, "What are you looking at today? Where is the focus of your attention? Are there challenges in your life to overcome? Don't just look at your problems as the days go by but look up to heaven. We must have faith in God. If you are always looking at your problems, feeling sorry for yourself, and telling everybody about them, you will become consumed by them. But class, when you look up to God and tell Him all about it, your life will start to move up. My Bible tells me that faith is what moves the hand of God! Keep your eyes and heart stayed on Jesus. Praise Him with your words and actions! Does anyone have something they would like to say?" she asked. The class was quiet! Lexie looked over at Effie and Effie looked at her mom. Effie raised her hand and said, "I would like to ask the Sunday School class to keep me in their prayers. I will be going away to school this fall. And, please, keep my parents in prayer. They need all the encouragement they can get.

I have truly enjoyed the lesson today," she said.

Church service stated at 11 a.m. The pastor opened service by singing one of his favorite hymns, "Stand Up for Jesus." Effie was at the piano. She played like she was at Carnegie Hall! Everyone stood and watched her fingers glide over the keyboard. The pastor left the pulpit and walked the aisles in the church. All the children were clapping, singing, and praising the Lord. The spirit was so high, they praised the Lord for 30 minutes or more. The pastor finally shared his text: Micah 3, "Do You Know Right from Wrong?"

Service ended at 2 p.m. The Hailey family walked home together. Hattie was expecting her Aunt Ollie for evening tea. The boys went their way and the girls sat around the house reading books.

It was now evening. Everyone was in the house and getting ready for another week. Effie would start her job at Miss Ann's house. She went to bed early so she would be on time for work.

Monday Morning

Effie was up and ready to go. She didn't have far to walk, so she took her time. She was there bright and early. As she was getting ready to knock on the back door, the door opened. Miss Ann's husband was standing in the kitchen and said, "Come in the house! I see you are a little early. Miss Ann will be out in a minute to show you where to start." Effie thanked him and stood on the doormat. She looked around the kitchen and then down the hallway, and thought to herself, "This kitchen ain't nothing compared to my momma's kitchen. Look at this wood floor. It ain't nothing! She thinks she's so rich and precious. God can take it all in a wink of an eye. These white folks think they are so special. They're no better than we are."

Miss Ann was watching Effie standing at the door. "Did you wipe your feet off before you came in?" she asked. Effie nodded. The only thing she wanted Miss Ann to tell her was where to start cleaning the house. "I'm leaving for work, now.

Have everything done when I get back. Start with the bedroom first, and then work your way to the kitchen," said Miss Ann.

Effie cleaned the bedrooms. Then she started on the bathroom. She washed the windows, mopped the floors, dusted the furniture in the living room. She took a break at noon. When she returned from lunch, she took the rugs out to beat the dust off them! It was getting close to 3 p.m. Miss Ann would be getting off work soon. Effie decided to mop the kitchen floor last. She got the mop and bucket. She looked at the clock and saw it was five minutes until 3 p.m. "Oh my," she thought. "She will be coming through that door any minute." She mopped everywhere except in front of the door. As she was mopping the last area, the door opened and Miss Ann yelled, "Oh no you didn't! Are you stupid? I know you're not mopping my floor with that mop! You know you're supposed to get on your knees and mop this wood floor." Effie looked at her with anger in her eyes. She forgot about the sermon on Sunday. She forgot about all the good things people said about her. She forgot about her sweet momma and good daddy. She put the mop in the bucket. Miss Ann grabbed the mop handle out of her hand and said, "You get down on your hands and knees. I have a brush for you to scrub this floor with." Effie looked at Miss Ann and said, "I don't get on my hands and knees for anybody, and I'm not stupid! If you want your floors scrubbed with someone's hands and knees, use your own! God gave you two of each." Effie opened the door and headed up the street toward home. She was so angry, hot tears poured down her cheeks like drops of rain. She walked so fast that she broke a sweat.

When she got home, her mother stood in the den ironing clothes. "What in the world's wrong with you?" she asked. Effie wiped the sweat from her forehead and sat down in a chair. "That woman is crazy! I'm not going back to that house. You know what she told me to do? She wanted me to get down on my knees and mop her stupid floor. What would I look like scrubbing that girl's floor? That's right, that girl, because she's the same age as me! She had to get married at 14 years old. Momma, you know it! Her husband got her pregnant and her momma made them get married. What do I look like taking orders from a woman my age, and a white woman, too?" Hattie rubbed Effie's back and told her it would be okay. She didn't have to go back.

"You wait until I see that gal! I'll get her told myself. Calling my youngster, stupid! I've been working for white people all my life, and none of them has never called me a name. I work for white people who got money! I always said, don't never work for these poor whites. They think they are better than you, but they're not. God made us from the dirt of the earth, and I have never seen white dirt unless it had some black mixed with it! We are either white or black, and there's nothing else in between!"

Lexie arrived at home about 5:30 p.m. that evening. His walk was about a mile from home. When he arrived, Effie was sitting in the dining room watching television. She fixed her father's dinner and put it on the dining room table. Lexie washed his hands and face and took off his shirt. After he said his blessings, he heard a knock at the front door. Effie got up and went to the door. To her surprise, it was Miss Ann!

She grabbed the door handle and walked in past Effie. She saw Lexie at the table eating his dinner, and yelled, "Uncle Lexie, do you know what Effie did to me today? She sassed me! I told her to get down on her knees and mop my floor and she got mad and talked back to me. I love you Uncle Lexie, and I will not stand for her to treat me that way! Now, what are you going to do about it?" When Effie heard what Miss Ann said, she got up and told her to leave their house. She voiced her opinion about how Miss Ann treated her. "Daddy, you don't have to say anything to this woman! She is getting out of here because I'm going to show her the door. And another thing! Stop calling my father Uncle Lexie! He is not your uncle!

My daddy may give you respect, but I don't have to respect anyone who doesn't respect me! And another thing! Give me my $2 for working in your house," she said angrily.

Miss Ann stormed out of Lexie and Hattie's house. She cried as she walked down the road. She could not believe that a colored girl was allowed to talk back to her as Effie did.

The next week, Effie went to pick cotton with some of her friends from school. She enjoyed going to the field. It gave her a chance to be with the other girls and to see Edward. The field owners were paying $1.50 per hundred pounds. Effie could easily pick 200-300 pounds each day. She worked for three months. The money she saved was for school and buying clothes for the winter.

September 1946, Livingstone College

Effie Louise Hailey finally arrived at 701 West Monroe Street, Salisbury North Carolina—Livingstone College. She was so excited. She was ready to meet new friends and prepare herself for all the classes in her major.

The library was her first stop. Andrew Carnegie Library was a special place at the school. She couldn't wait to study and do research for some of her classes. "There's Ballard Hall! That's the name of one of my streets in Wadesboro!" she said, excitedly. She found her room and unpacked her things. Later, one of the girls who she saw in the hallway came to her room. "Hi, my name is Deborah, what's yours, may I ask?" Effie introduced herself and offered to help the girl with her bags. They shook hands and got ready to go to an assembly in the gym. Everyone was there.

Three Months Later

Effie was excited about going home for the Christmas holiday. She wanted to see her parents. All the church members would be excited to hear her play the piano again. She missed home badly, but if she would make something out of herself, she had to leave Wadesboro. One special person she wanted to see was Edward. "I hope he comes home for the holiday," thought Effie. "Well, if he doesn't come home, maybe he's found a beautiful girl at A&T! I'm not the only girl in the world. There's a lot of pretty girls out there, and a man will be a man. I'm not going to think that way! I'll just wait and see if he'll come looking for me," she thought.

Effie was on the Greyhound Express Bus. She didn't want the bus to take her to her address, so she asked the driver to drop her off on Salisbury Street. There were beautiful homes on Salisbury Street. She wanted to impress her friends. She wanted them to think she lived in one of those beautiful, white houses. When she got off the bus, she grabbed her bags and walked to her aunt's house. When she looked back at the bus, the girls were waving and saying, "Goodbye, see you later, Effie!"

Aunt Nina was standing in her living room. She saw Effie coming to the porch. She opened the door and said, "Girl, where are you coming from? I didn't know who you were. Come on in the house and put your bags down. Do you need to call your momma and Lexie?" Effie walked in and gave Aunt Nina a hug. "I got off here because I didn't want then to see my street. It's small and some of the houses need to be painted." Aunt Nina looked at Effie and said, "You mean to tell me that you are ashamed of the street you live on? Effie, you listen to me! Your momma and daddy worked hard to keep that roof over your head. I bet some of those kids on that bus live in worse places than yours. And you know what, I bet they are not ashamed of it, either! You listen to me, and you listen well! Don't you ever be ashamed of where you come from. I don't care who it is, you tell them good things about your town and the street you live on. Be proud of your family! It will go well with you, you hear me?" Effie was hurt that she felt that way. She didn't mean for Aunt Nina to get angry, but she was telling the truth. She made her mind up, she would get off at her house the next time.

She walked across the street to go

home. When she got there, she saw that her brother, Lucius, was home from the Army. She was so glad to see him. They hugged and started talking about Salisbury and the war. Lucius was thankful to be home. He was waiting for his brother, Walter, who would be delayed for a day or two.

Hattie and Lexie were proud of their children. They had one in the Navy and another one was going a few months later. One daughter was in college and another daughter would graduate from high school soon after.

Later that evening, Lucius and Effie wanted to go out for a while. It had been a long time since they saw their friends. The only place jumping was Hammond's Café. It was near their house, so they washed up, changed into some comfortable clothes, and walked across the street.

When Lucius opened the door to the café, the girls got out of control and screamed so loudly, the owner of the café' put the closed sign on the window. There wasn't any room for the people who were coming in. "Please, please, you all! Give him some space. The man can't breathe! He's not going anywhere for a while. He's home now. It will be enough of him to go around. I promise! Let the man get some air!" said the owner. The girls sat down at the bar. Lucius introduced Effie. "Listen up! This is my sister, Effie. She's back from college for the Christmas holidays. I want everybody here to get a drink on me tonight! I love all of you!" When he said that, a beautiful light skinned, tall, slim girl walked to the bar. She was in the back of the café with her uncle and aunt. Lucius was speechless! He looked at the girl from head to toe. He hunched Effie on the arm, and said, "You see that girl? That is going to be my wife!" Effie looked at him and said, "You must be crazy! You don't even know her name."

January 2, 1946

Christmas was over. Effie went back to college and the boys got jobs to help with the family. Lucius worked with his father at the school, and Walter went to a trade school to become a carpenter. The Hailey family owned cars and they remodeled the house and did other improvements for the home.

Effie wrote a letter every week to her parents. She wanted to keep up with the boys and wanted to know if her sister was ready for graduation from high school. On the weekends, she would catch the bus to Greensboro to see Edward. They were in love and nothing could separate those two from each other.

1947

Effie came home in June to get a job. She wanted to work somewhere better than the cotton fields and someone's house. She wanted to work in a store, but where would that be? "Maybe a café," she thought.

A whole month went by, and she found nothing at all to do. "Well, I guess I can work at the church and play for them. Maybe, another church in town will hire me to play for them too." The Methodist

Church was the only church that needed a player. So she picked cotton during the week and played the piano on Sundays. She made enough money for clothes, shoes, and books for the next year.

August 1948

Effie worked hard at school. Going back and forth to Greensboro to see Edward was getting to be expensive.

One morning, Effie wasn't feeling well. She decided to go to the infirmary to see the doctor. She didn't have any energy to go to class. She was sick to her stomach for several mornings. She didn't know what it was. She sat on the side of her bed and thought, "Maybe it's a virus or something I ate in the school cafeteria!"

The next morning, she had an appointment with the school doctor. She walked in the office and the nurse called her name to come forward. "Miss Hailey, how long have you been feeling this way?" she asked. Effie thought about it for a moment, "I guess for over a week. I feel like I have eaten something that wasn't good for me."

The nurse asked Effie to come in the examining room, passed her a gown, and asked her to remove all her clothes. "Have you been sexually active, young lady?" Effie was ashamed to answer.

She knew she and Edward had been intimate several times in the last few months. "Yes, I have," said Effie. The nurse gave Effie a cup to catch her urine in. "Go to the bathroom and pee in this cup. Bring it back to me and I'll see what the results are," said the nurse. Effie did as she was asked. She waited outside the examining room for 30 minutes. Finally, the nurse called her name and asked her to come in and have a seat. The doctor came in with the nurse, and said, "Young lady, you are pregnant. You will deliver your baby in May of next year. If there are any complications with your pregnancy, you could deliver earlier this year. Do you have any questions for us at this time?" Effie shook her head.

She left the clinic in tears. "What in

the world am I going to do? This is my second year in school! I can't quit now! I must tell Momma and Daddy soon! What are they going to think of me, now?" She thought about all these 'what if's' before heading to her room.

Chapter 2

• • •

Effie stayed in her room. She closed the curtains and opened a magazine with pictures of newlywed couples in it. "I don't know what to do. I must let Edward know about the baby. Who should I tell first, my parents or Edward?" she thought. Either way, it would be a difficult situation. Edward was going to school to better himself, and her parents had their hopes built so high for her. She didn't want to let anyone down.

Effie couldn't sleep. She tossed and turned in her bed. Her first class began at 8 a.m. and she needed her rest. Finally, she dozed off. Suddenly, there was a knock at her door. She thought she was dreaming. "Who is it?" she yelled. It was one of her friends from class. "Effie! Are you alright in there?" she asked, while holding her ear to the door. Effie jumped out of bed and ran to the door. "Yes, I'm okay. What time is it?" she asked her friend. The young lady told her that it was almost 8 a.m. and their class would be starting soon. Effie thanked the girl for waking her up. "You go on without me. I so sorry that you had to wake me up. I'll explain everything to you later." The girl went to class and Effie got ready to go talk to the Dean of Students.

It was around noon and Effie was sitting in the hallway waiting for her turn to see the Dean. She was feeling bad about her problem, but she still felt excited at the same time. "I want my baby! If I must leave school and get a job, then, that's what I'll do," she thought. She knew her dad would be disappointed, but her mom would be excited about Effie's pregnancy. Effie's parents always stressed to their children how important it was to graduate from school. They wanted all of them to be able to take care of themselves and get a good job. Their future would be different from when their parents grew up. The cotton fields were plentiful, but soon manufacturing plants would be built to process the cotton, and education would play a huge part in getting a job. Farmers were selling their crops to the local grocery stores, and to work in a store, you had to know how to read, write and count money. Lexie and Hattie wanted the best for their children. They made sure that the boys worked after school, and the girls learned to work at home. Effie knew how her parents were. She didn't want to disappoint them. She was smart and could always go back to school after she had the baby. "I know what I'll do. I'm going to let the Dean know that I'm pregnant and I'm going to have my baby. I'm going to leave school, and that's final," she thought.

October 1947

Maple Lane was the same and so were the people. Effie got off the Greyhound Bus in front of her house. Hattie met her at the driveway. She was still proud of her daughter. She helped Effie with her bags and hugged her as they walked to the front door. "Come on in, Baby! You can have the front room!" she said, as she put all the bags on the bed. Effie sat down on the bed, and said, "Momma, I'm sorry to disappoint you and Daddy. I know you have high hopes for me. You know how much I love Edward. It was a mistake on my part." Her mother looked at her, and said, "No! It takes two people to get a baby! You let him know what he did, too!" Effie held her head down and said, "You're right, Momma! I'll get in touch with him and let him know. He still thinks I'm at Livingstone!"

Late that night, she decided to write Edward a letter. She wanted to meet somewhere so they could talk privately, but the timing may have been a problem for him. "Writing letters to someone is not my thing to do. I like talking to a person to their face. I can't do it. I just can't do it!" she said, as she tore the paper into tiny pieces. "I'll call him tomorrow and tell him about the baby. Then, it will be all over," she thought.

• • •

Effie woke up at 7 a.m. the next morning with Edward on her mind. She looked in her purse for his number. She took the phone into the bedroom. "Hello, Edward. Are you up, yet?" she asked. "Effie? Uh, yeah. What's going on?" he asked sleepily. "I'm not going to talk long. I wanted you to know that I had to leave Livingstone. I'm pregnant with your baby. The doctor said I will have it next spring, I think in May," she said, listening for his response.

Edward was heartbroken. He didn't want Effie to drop out of school. He knew how much going to college meant to her and her parents. But on the other hand, being a father made him feel special. "Effie, let me know how you are doing. I want to call you every month, and if I can help in any way, you let me know," he said. The two said their goodbyes and expressed their love for one another. Effie sat quietly in her room. She prayed to God to show her what to do. "Whatever you want me to do, I'll do it Lord!" she prayed.

The following week, Effie asked for her job at the church. She missed playing the piano. She worked in the cotton fields with her friends during the week and played the piano on Sundays and for special occasions.

Her oldest brother announced his engagement to Olivia, the girl he met at the café. Everyone was excited about the news. He would live near Coley Hill until he could build his own house. Effie liked her brother's girlfriend and they became very close. They talked about the baby and read books about taking care of an infant and the mother's health during pregnancy. "How many children do you want?" Effie asked. Olivia looked at Effie and said, "I want a boy and a girl!"

April 1949

Effie's brothers were getting married in South Carolina. The Hailey family would get two additions to their family because Walter was getting married too. The Hailey boys loved beautiful women. "Where did y'all find these pretty women? I didn't know Wadesboro had such good looking girls," their father said.

After the wedding, everyone decided to go to the Hailey's home for supper.

Effie played the piano and the boys sang the blues, laughed, and had fun.

It was getting late, so the boys took their wives home. The next day would be a challenge for the husbands. Lucius and Walter had jobs at Wadesboro High School in town. They knew they needed to do whatever they could to provide for their families. Their wives didn't have jobs, and the only work they knew how to do was pick cotton.

Early Monday Morning

The next day, Effie woke early. She had an appointment at the Anson County Health Department. The clinic was about three miles from where she lived. On her way to the clinic, she had to pass the Watson's home. There was a man standing in the front door. He watched as Effie walked by. He yelled out the door, "Hello, there." Effie looked up and waved.

Soon Effie arrived at the clinic. "Mother, you must eat nutritious foods for your baby. Read books and talk to your baby. You are doing a good job on your weight," the nurse told Effie.

On her way back home, she saw the young man who was standing in the Watson's front door. "Hey, aren't you the girl who lives in the Hailey home?" he asked. Effie looked back at him and said, "Yes."

"My name is George! What's yours?" he asked. Effie told him who she was and tried to walk a little faster to avoid him. He wouldn't let up. He walked just as fast as she did. "I just want to talk to you! I'm a nice guy. I know your brothers, Lucius and Walter!" he said. Effie stopped in her tracks and looked at him. She didn't know what to say. Being rude wasn't in her nature. "Well, it's nice to meet you, George," said Effie.

The two walked together down Maple Lane. George talked about the war and Effie talked about Livingstone College. When they reached their destinations, George asked Effie if he could come visit some-times. Effie accepted his invitation and told him Wednesday nights would be fine.

A few months later, George told Effie that he was going to New Jersey to work in the new Campbell Soup plant. "Jobs are plentiful in New Jersey. I would like to live there and have a family someday," he told Effie. She wished him well and said goodbye.

May was coming soon, and Effie was ready to have her baby. Her mother was excited about the arrival of her first grandchild. The two would sit and talk for hours. Hattie wanted to know what she would do when the baby came but Effie was undecided about her future. "Momma, I want to stay with you after the baby comes. I don't know how to be a mother!" Her mother looked at her and said, "I know you don't know, but God will teach you what to do." Hattie was glad to hear her say she wanted to stay at home with the baby. She loved babies and thought she was the only one who could take better care of them.

...

Effie was overweight and didn't follow the nurse's advice. She was miserable! Her feet were swollen, and the other parts of her body were too. She couldn't rest in the bed, and she couldn't sit comfortably in a chair. She complained about the weather and the noise that her younger brother was making. So, she decided to go walking. She went to see her sister-in-law, Olivia. The two young women had become good friends.

Olivia had some good news to tell Effie. "I'm going to have a baby, too," she said. They hugged and Effie started crying happy tears. The only thing she could think about at that moment was that her parents were going to get their blessings. Grandchildren were on their way!

May 25, 1949

Effie was in labor. She had been up all night long. Her mother stayed by her bedside and rubbed her back and massaged her head. They called the doctor earlier, but he had an emergency across town. Miss Sis Watson was a midwife for many mothers in the county. "Go get Miss Sis!" her mother told one of the boys. Soon Miss Sis was walking down the road. When she got to the house, she didn't knock, she just entered and yelled, "Where is she? Do you have some hot water and some towels?"

Hattie didn't have time to greet her. She got the hot water and towels. "The doctor is on his way," she told Miss Sis. The two women calmed Effie as the pain continued to increase. "She's going to have this baby in a minute. We can't wait on the doctor," said Miss Sis. Hattie got down on her knees to say a prayer for her daughter. At that moment, she looked up and saw the head of the baby coming. "I see it. Lord, I see the head coming out!" she yelled. Miss Sis grabbed the towel and helped the baby to a safe delivery. "Here comes the doctor!" one of the boys yelled.

"This is a fine gal," said Miss Sis. Suddenly, the doctor came in with his bag. He cut the umbilical cord and gave the baby to Hattie for a thorough cleansing. The doctor weighed the baby and asked, "What are you naming this child?" Effie looked at the doctor and said, "Her name is Margaret Marie Hailey." The doctor wrote the baby's name and weight in his record book. He congratulated Effie and told the family to take good care of the baby.

Effie stayed in bed for the rest of

the night. Hattie held the baby in her arms and asked the Lord to take care of her grandchild. She rubbed the baby's black curly hair. She searched the baby all over, making sure all the body parts were intact. She rubbed the baby's legs and arms. Then, Effie opened her eyes and asked for her daughter. She began to nurse the baby. As she held her, there was an instant bond of love. Tears ran down her cheeks, and she said, "Momma, isn't she beautiful? Look at the curls in her hair!"

Hattie and Lexie couldn't stay away from Effie's bedroom. "Why did you name her Margaret?" her father asked. Effie tried to explain that a name should mean something. "Daddy, the name Margaret means that she's a pearl. She is a child of light—mighty, strong, soft and gentle, and ambitious. I wanted my baby's name to be special!" Her father looked at her and said, "I like that!"

One Month Later

Effie was confused about why her

baby cried so much. She fed the baby every few hours like her mother told her to do, but the baby cried as if she was in pain. Her mother gave the baby a spoon full of her special tea, thinking it was her stomach. She rubbed the baby's back and made sure she burped after each feeding. Nothing seemed to work! "Momma, this isn't normal for a baby to cry like this!" Effie cried.

The next day, Effie and Hattie took the baby to the doctor. As they waited for the doctor, the baby cried even more. Effie tried to console the baby, but nothing she did would work. Her mother decided to give it another try but it didn't help.

A nurse finally came to the door and asked Effie to bring her baby in. The two women went into the examining room with the baby. "What's going on with this baby?" the doctor asked. Effie began to tell him about the baby crying all the time. He asked several questions to try to understand what might be wrong.

"Well, let me see here. This baby is beautiful! Look at these curly locks on her head! And what beautiful eyes she has. I have never seen a Negro baby with blue eyes! This is so unusual! If I wasn't looking at her myself, I wouldn't have believed it!" he said. The doctor made his final report. He told Effie and her mom that he would refer her to a specialist in Charlotte, North Carolina. He would make the appointment, and they had to be there the next day. Effie thanked the doctor and she and her mother left for home.

The next day Effie and her brother got up early. The appointment was at 1 p.m. She dressed her baby in a pretty outfit. White and blue were Effie's favorite colors. The baby wore black patent leather shoes with white laced socks. She knew everyone would say something nice about her, so she made sure she and her baby were well-dressed.

They arrived at the doctor's office. Effie took the elevator to the third floor of the building. She walked to the office door and a nurse opened it and asked her to come in. When they called her name, she took the baby in and greeted the doctor. She told him all about her baby and wanted to know if he could help her.

The doctor took the baby in his arms. "My, oh my, this is a beautiful baby!" He began to examine the baby from head to toe. When he put her clothes back on, he noticed something odd. "Who is this baby's father?" Effie looked at him and said, "Her daddy's name is Edward Elliot. Why do you ask?" The doctor told Effie that it was strange to see a Negro baby with blue eyes. "I'm going to look in the back of her eyes. There's got to be an answer for this." He looked in the baby's eyes and said, "Yes! There's something behind her right eye that doesn't belong there!" He decided to go across the hall to another doctor and ask if he would come over to look at the baby. "This is a specialist for babies, Miss Hailey. I want him to look at your baby and see what he thinks." The doctor looked at the baby and said, "There's a tumor behind this child's eye and she needs to have it taken out. If not, then she may lose it."

Tears rolled down Effie's face. She didn't want her baby to be operated on. The doctors told Effie that the surgery would be the next week and there would only be a small incision in the back of her head. "I will make the appointment, Miss Hailey. Don't worry! We will take good care of your baby!" the doctor said.

The following week, the Hailey family prepared themselves for the trip to Charlotte. Effie got up that morning and dressed her baby. She didn't know what the outcome would be, so she and her mother said a prayer while her father and brothers loaded the car. "Lord, you know all about my baby. I want you to cover her with your mercy like you did for others. Be with her on the operating table. Guide the doctors' hands and give them the knowledge to heal and repair anything that is wrong with her. Take care of us on the dangerous highway. Bless the people who we are about to meet and take care of the ones we leave behind. In your precious name we pray, Amen!"

The family arrived at Charlotte Memorial Hospital at 8 a.m. As they rode up the elevator, Effie held her baby as tightly as she could. She wanted to be brave and not cry, but her emotions took over.

"Mom, I don't want them to cut my baby!" she said softly. Hattie put her arms around her and said, "Trust God. Just trust God."

The nurse told the family to wait in the waiting area. The surgery would take about an hour and the recovery time was the same. She offered them coffee and snacks as they waited, but they refused to eat or drink. The only thing they wanted was for the surgery to be over so they could get on the road for home.

Chapter 3

· · ·

The baby was in recovery and was doing well. Effie couldn't wait to see her. She paced the floor while waiting for the nurse to come through the door. Finally, the door opened. It was the doctor. "Well, Miss Hailey, the operation was a success. No complications. She's asleep now. I want you to take her home and watch her very carefully for the next month or so. Bring her back if there's any problems," he said. Effie and her mother thanked him and the nurses for all they had done.

The family was on their way back to Wadesboro. Effie uncovered her baby and looked at her scar. "They shaved a little spot on my baby's head!" she cried.

They arrived home safely. Effie got out of the car and went into the house. She laid the baby on her mom's bed and sat down in a chair. "Momma," she said. "I hope we don't have to take her back to Charlotte. I have a funny feeling about this surgery." Her mother looked at her and said, "Put it all in God's hands. He will work it out!"

There was a knock at the front door. It was their neighbor, Miss Alice. She wanted to see the baby. She walked in the bedroom and pulled the covers off the baby. The baby was awake and smiled at her. "Oh my! Look at that! She is a beautiful baby! And look at those eyes. You know, old people use to say, a baby with blue eyes can't see. But this baby is looking at me and smiling, too!" Hattie was furious! Why did Alice say that, especially since they were just getting home from the hospital? "Yes, she can see you and she can see us too. I think it's time for you to go, Alice!" Miss Alice apologized. She didn't know about the baby's condition, but Hattie wasn't going to hear it. She knew the baby was in God's care and that was that.

...

Three Months Later

Effie was working for Miss Ann again. She needed more money, and since she lived down the road from her house, she decided to work for her on the weekends and pick cotton in the mornings.

One morning when she got out of bed, she looked to see if the baby was asleep. When she pulled the covers back, she saw blood on the side of the baby's face. She yelled for her mother and said, "Look! The baby's eye is bleeding. What's happening to my baby?" Hattie picked up the baby and said, "Call the doctor!"

•••

The two women arrived at the doctor's office with the baby. The doctor looked at the baby and said, "She's got to go back to the hospital!" It was a sad night for the Hailey family. Little Margaret had to go into surgery again. The stiches came loose and caused her eye to hemorrhage.

It was so badly damaged that it had to be removed. Effie and her mother were devastated. Effie didn't want to hear of it, but she knew in her heart it was best for her baby. "My baby can live a happy life with one eye. I'm going to make sure of that!" she cried.

Baby Margaret stayed in the hospital for a week. All the nurses and doctors enjoyed taking care of her. She was a good baby. She smiled a lot and tried to talk back to the nurses. They bought toys for her. The scar didn't make Effie love the baby any less. She prayed that the Lord would take care of her baby, and He did!

Finally, she was home from the hospital. All the neighbors and other family members came to see her. No one asked about her eye. They were too excited about her beautiful curly black hair. Miss Sis came to see her too. "This is a fine beautiful gal you have here. Let me hold her, I want to bless and lay hands on her!" Miss Sis lifted her off the bed. She prayed a prayer that went straight to God! She laid her hands on the baby's head, heart, arms, and legs. "Alright, now let God do His work!"

When Miss Sis left the house, everyone was praising God and singing hymns. There was not a dry eye in the house. Hattie knew everything would be alright. She trusted God a long time ago. Her faith was built on the solid rock, Jesus, and no other! She knew she had to be strong for her daughter. The future would be challenging, but Hattie was ready to do anything and go anywhere for her first grand baby.

Three Years Later

The baby had to go back to Charlotte for a follow-up visit. When Effie and Hattie arrived, the doctor asked them to bring her to the examining room. He looked in her eyes and discovered her sight in her other eye was also failing. He hesitated before speaking. He looked up to the ceiling, then bowed his head and said, "Miss Hailey, your baby is blind. She doesn't have sight in either eye. I don't know what happened! It's beyond anything I have ever seen." Tears flowed down Effie's face. She held her baby tightly in her arms. Hattie put her hands on the baby's head and said, "This is the work of God!"

One day, Effie had to go in town. She walked up Maple Lane Street to get to Salisbury Street. As she was walking past the Watson's house, George was sitting on the porch. "Hey there!" he said. Effie looked up and saw him smiling at her. "Can I walk with you? I don't have anything else to do." Effie smiled and said he could and they both walked towards town.

"Are you seeing anyone, Effie? I mean, do you have a boyfriend or are you engaged?" he asked. She looked at him and said, "No." He smiled and said, "I like you a lot! I would love to come see you and the baby. By the way, how is she?" She told him that her daughter was fine, and that he could come visit them. George was so happy. He was lonely and wanted a nice girl to someday marry and have a family with.

On the way back home, he carried Effie's bags, and they laughed and talked about things that were going on in the neighborhood. As the weeks and months went by, they became very close. George wanted to know how much Effie really cared for him. He had plans to go to New Jersey and get a job at the Campbell Soup Company. He wanted to get married and leave Wadesboro. So, that Wednesday night, he decided to ask Effie's father for her hand in marriage. He knew how Lexie was about his children, so he had to be very careful. Effie and that baby were his pride and joy.

Wednesday Night at the Hailey's House

George got dressed and walked down the road to Effie's house. He had rehearsed what he would say. "Mr. Lexie, I want to marry Effie! No. Mr. Lexie, Effie and I are in love, and we are going to get married. No! I can't say it that way! I know, I'll just ask Effie would she marry me, and leave it like that!" he thought.

He walked inside. Effie was sitting in the front room holding her daughter. "Come on in, George!" she said. George sat down on the sofa. He moved over near Effie and the baby. "Can I hold her?" he asked. She gave him the girl and at once, she started playing with his watch. "I think she likes me!" he said to Effie. "Can she talk?" Effie fixed the girls dress and said, "Why don't you ask her!" George asked the child for her name, and to his surprise she said, "Margaret Marie!"

Later that night, George asked Effie to marry him. She accepted. He told her all about his plans to move to New Jersey. Effie wanted a new start too, and she was excited to move to the north and get away from Wadesboro.

The next day, she told her dad that she and George were getting married. Lexie was not happy! He wanted her to stay home, get a better job and go back to school. Effie tried to explain to him the benefits of leaving the country and moving to the city. But her dad wouldn't listen. He told her that she wasn't going to take the baby anywhere. They argued for hours. When her mom got a chance to speak, she looked at Effie and said, "Alright, you can go, but you must leave the child with me. I will take care of the baby. You go to New Jersey, get a job and you send us money and clothes for your child. When she is old enough, you can come get her, if she wants to go!"

Effie agreed. Although she didn't want to leave her baby, she knew she had to go in order to better herself and provide for her daughter.

Chapter 4

. . .

1952, Camden, New Jersey

The bus ride to Camden was exciting. Effie saw the tall, nice apartment buildings. "George?" she asked. "Are we going to get a house or an apartment?" George looked at her and said, "We will find an apartment or get one of the row houses in Camden's south side." She didn't know what a row house was, but she trusted her husband to make her happy.

Effie and George were so in love. He wanted her to be happy. It didn't matter to him where they lived. He was married now and that was that!

His relatives were expecting them to arrive sometime later that night. George looked at his watch and smiled at Effie. "Are you hungry?" he asked. "We are almost at our destination! My brother will be up waiting on us." Effie nodded. George decided to get off the bus on Cooper Street and get a bite to eat at the Bistro Restaurant. He and Effie didn't stay long, because the streets were crowded, and he feared for their safety.

The couple walked about two blocks and there was the house. That was Effie's first-time seeing houses together in rows. She looked at George and held his arm tightly. "Come on, Effie!" he said, "This is it!" They walked up the four stairs onto the porch. George knocked on the door. Before he could knock again, a man opened the door and yelled, "Hey, man! Come on in!" George greeted the man and introduced him to his wife. The man grabbed Effie and said, "Hey there, sister-in-law! I'm glad to meet you. Come on in and rest yourselves." George and Effie sat on the sofa. Effie asked to go to the restroom. George directed her to the stairs and opened the door. As he was walking back to his seat, he looked in a bedroom that was decorated with new furniture. When he turned to go sit down, he asked, "Is that our room on the left side of the hallway?" His brother confirmed that it was. "I wanted you to have something nice for your new bride, so I bought that bedroom suit at a warehouse downtown," said his brother. George thanked him and reassured him that he would pay rent and keep everything nice and clean. Effie was tired and wanted to rest. She asked if she could take a bath and go to bed. George gave her towels and unpacked their bags.

Effie got up early the next day. She wanted to walk downtown to see the city. She asked George to walk with her. He got his hat and jacket. He looked around the room for the newspaper. "I'm going to check out some jobs while we're in town," he said. Effie said it was okay, and they walked for about a mile. Effie looked at the skyscrapers. She looked at more houses in the neighborhood. It wasn't what she expected. The only time she saw the city was on television. She didn't realize that it would be crowded with so many people. Everyone was walking fast. Cars and trucks, taxi cabs and street cars raced by. It was too much for this country girl!

George and Effie applied for jobs at the Campbell Soup Company. They were both hired and were set to start the next week! Everything was going well for the Watson couple. In a month's time they bought new furniture and moved into their own two-bedroom house.

Effie called her parents often to see how her little girl was doing. Her mother would always say the same thing, "Don't you worry about this child. She is fine."

The Next Month

Effie was addicted to shopping. She found a department store that sold children's clothes. When she got paid on Fridays, she would go to the store and shop for her little girl. The clerk knew her when she entered the door. "May I help you, Mrs. Watson?" she asked Effie. She smiled at the lady and said, "Oh, I'm looking for dresses for my little girl!" The lady showed Effie what they had on sale. Effie walked to the sale racks. She was amazed at the prices. She bought a blue dress with a coat and hat to match. There was a sailor's outfit for a girl that she just had to buy, along with four more dresses that would be perfect for church. In all her shopping, she saved enough money to buy something for herself.

The next day, she packed the clothes in a box and mailed them to 811 Maple Lane Street.

Saturday Morning

Hattie met the mailman at the road. He greeted her and said, "Hattie, here's your package from your daughter! It's got to be something for that beautiful little grand of yours." Hattie thanked him and went inside the house. She laid the box on the floor. "Margaret!" she called. "Come, open your box!"

Little Margaret tried to sit on the box. Then she smiled at her grandma and tried to pick up the box. "Wait a minute! Let me remove the tape so you can open it!" said Hattie. Margaret stood back as Hattie helped open the flaps. When Margaret reached her little hands in the box, she pulled out the blue dress and hat. She felt the dress with her fingers. She held the hat to her nose to smell the fabric. "This is mine!" she smiled. Hattie removed the other dresses from the box. "Look Margaret! You have five dresses, a coat that matches and a hat and shoulder bag, too. Your mother is spending all her money on her baby!" Margaret sat down on the floor and tried to hold all her clothes in her arms. "What color is this one, and this one, Momma?" Hattie called out all the colors as Margaret enjoyed her gifts from her mom.

Every time Hattie and the family took their first grand out in public, she was fancily dressed. People in town and in church made a fuss over that little girl who looked like a living doll. Lexie wouldn't have any other way. He loved that baby girl!

He was so protective of her. If she stumbled over a chair, Lexie would scold the boys and Hattie. He didn't want her to fall. When she played with her toys, someone had to be right there with her.

"Don't step on her fingers!" he would yell.

Saturday Night

Effie and George called to see if Margaret received her package. "Mom, how is my baby girl?" asked Effie. The answer was always the same. "Don't you worry about this child. Take care of yourself and keep working," her mother said.

Two Years Later

Margaret was now five years old. One day, Hattie went to the mailbox. There was a letter from the State School for the Blind. The principal wanted to visit with the guardians of Margaret Marie Hailey. The letter stated that he would be in Wadesboro on the following Monday, and the time to expect him. Hattie told Lexie about the letter. "Ah, what did he say, woman?" Hattie tried to explain to her husband that Margaret was school age now, and she had to go to school like all the other children. But Lexie didn't agree.

"That baby can't see! You mean to tell me she got to go to school anyway?" Margaret heard everything. She wanted to be with other children her age. Her cousin was her age, and the other ones were younger.

She sat on the floor and turned her head to hear more. "Well Lexie, the man is coming Monday. He wants to talk to both of us. You just be quiet and let me handle this! What do you want the child to do? Sit here with us for the rest of her life? That's not going to happen. Just because she is blind, doesn't mean she can't learn. She's almost six years old and can understand better than some children who can see. Let the Lord have His way with this child!" Lexie would not argue with Hattie. Whenever she added God in their arguments, God always won!

August 1955

Hattie was cleaning the house for their visitor. The principal was coming at 2 p.m. that afternoon. She dressed Margaret in one of her prettiest outfits and told her to sit on the sofa in the living room so she wouldn't get dirty.

At that time, there was a knock at the door. Hattie greeted the man and asked him to come in. "Hello, Ma'am! My name is Mr. Crockett. I'm the principal at the School for the Blind in Raleigh, North Carolina. Now, who do I owe the pleasure?" he asked. "I'm Hattie Hailey, the child's grandmother. Come on in and have a seat," said Hattie.

Mr. Crockett sat on the sofa near the child. "Hello there! Now what's your name?" he asked. Margaret sat with her legs hanging off the sofa and answered, "Margaret Marie!" Mr. Crockett touched the girl's hand and said he was glad to meet her. "I bet you are eager to go to school and play with other boys and girls your age!" Margaret tugged at the hem of her dress and answered, "Yes! When can I go?" Mr. Crockett was surprised! He thought that Margaret would cry and say she didn't want to leave her grandparents. "School starts the last of this month. If you are ready, I'm here to welcome you to your kindergarten class."

Margaret reached over to feel who she was talking to. She rubbed his coat sleeve and then down to his hand. "You are a very smart girl! Mrs. Hailey, there's another young lady from this area who attends our school, also. Her name is Freddie. I was wondering if you knew any of her people!" he said. Hattie nodded and said, "Yes! I know the family. I heard they had a blind daughter." Mr. Crockett thought it would be a great idea for the girls to meet some day. He turned to Margaret and asked, "Do you have any questions for me?" Margaret turned her head and smiled. She touched his hand again and asked, "Do you have a merry-go-round at your school?" He looked at Hattie and smiled, "Yes, we do! We have swings, sliding boards, and sandboxes, too!" Margaret didn't say another word. She smiled and rubbed the man's arm as he talked to her grandma. When the meeting was over, Hattie signed all the necessary papers for Margaret to enroll in school.

Later that night, she called Effie

and told her the good news. Everyone was excited except Lexie. He didn't want to see his grand baby going that far away to school. But if Hattie and the mother thought it was alright, he would go along with their decision. Arguing about it wouldn't make a difference.

Chapter 5

. . .

August 30, 1955

Hattie washed and packed all of Margaret's clothes. She tried not to forget anything, so she made a list of items. Everything was checked off her list. Margaret was sitting at the dining room table and asked her grandmother, "Can we have snacks on our trip?" Hattie looked at her and said, "I forgot about snacks! What would you like to snack on?" Margaret turned her head and said, "I want some chips and two Baby Ruth's, and some drinks, and don't forget my doll!" Hattie made sure everything she wanted was packed and ready to go.

Early, the next morning, the Hailey family loaded all their luggage in the trunk of the car. Robert drove. Lexie sat in the front passenger side. Ray, Hattie, and Margaret had the back seat. This trip would take a while. They had to cross the Pee Dee River bridge, travel on to Rockingham, then to Southern Pines, and on to Highway 1 North. They stopped for bathroom breaks and gas. When they stopped, Lexie got out to buy his favorite snack—a pound cake and a pop soda. Hattie and Margaret opened their bags and ate what they packed. The boys exchanged drivers in Southern Pines. They still had a long way to go.

Finally, around noon, the Haileys reached their destination—Garner, North Carolina. Lexie was sitting up in his seat reading the signs. "There is it! State School for the Blind and Deaf! Ah, this, this here is a big place!" he said. Hattie sat quietly in the back seat looking at the school. Lexie and Ray got out to stretch their legs. The campus was huge and there were a lot of children walking back and forth from one building to the next.

Hattie wanted to see if there were any adults walking with the children, but most of the children were walking alone with other children. She looked to the left side of the building and saw two teenage girls walking together. As the girls got near the car, Hattie got out and asked for direction. She noticed that the girls were blind. "Excuse me," she said. "My name is Hattie Mae Hailey!" The girls stopped. One of them asked, "Are you Mrs. Hattie Mae Hailey from Wadesboro?" Hattie said she was. "My name is Freddie, and this is my friend, Geraldine. My mother told me that you had a granddaughter who was coming to this school! It's nice to meet you! And what is your grand-daughter's name?" she asked. Margaret was listening to the conversation, and yelled out, "My name is Margaret Marie Hailey!" Freddie told Margaret that she was pleased to meet her. She and Geraldine offered their hands to greet her. Hattie asked Freddie to visit Margaret whenever she was free. The two girls said they would be glad to check on her.

They directed Hattie to the main office, but when she turned and looked up, she said, "I see a sign that says,

Admissions. I think that's where we supposed to go!" She held Margaret's hand and walked across the lawn. As they approached the building, a young man came to the door and greeted them. "Come on in. You must be the Hailey family! Mr. Crockett is expecting you!" he said.

Hattie and Margaret went into the office. She signed more papers and was assisted by a young woman. "Hello, my name is Miss Haywood! I am the House Mother for the kindergarten class," she said. Miss Haywood shook Hattie's hand and reached down to greet Margaret. "You must be Margaret! I have heard so much about you. Do you remember the man who came to see you in Wadesboro?" she asked. Margaret nodded.

Miss Haywood asked the family to walk with her to the kindergarten dormitory. Hattie was the only one who wanted to go. She carried the bags and told the men to wait for her in the car. Miss Haywood held Margaret's hand. She wanted her to meet the student who would assist her on campus. "Margaret, I want you to meet Carolyn. She is a second grader. She will take you to the cafeteria, your classroom, and out on the playground doing recess. You will not go anywhere unless Carolyn is with you. Do you understand?" she asked. Margaret nodded.

Carolyn greeted Margaret. She wanted to know about some of her favorite things to do. She offered to take Margaret to meet her classmates, but Miss Haywood stopped her. "Let her stay with her parents for now, and you can go after dinner!" The girls held hands and walked in front of the adults.

After about an hour, it was time to say goodbye. Hattie hugged Margaret and told her that everything would be okay. Margaret didn't seem to mind her family leaving. She had a friend, a playground, and a place to learn new things. She was happy to start going to school.

"You be good! If you want to call home, you know the number!" her grandma said. "Yes ma'am, I know the number!" said Margaret, as she proudly recited the telephone number. Hattie hugged her one more time. She looked around for the car. She didn't want Margaret to know she was crying. "Okay! We're going back home. Call if you need me!" Margaret happily walked away with her new friend, Carolyn.

Monday Morning, First Day of School

Carolyn went to the dormitory to get Margaret. She was dressed and ready to go. She told Margaret to always stay on the sidewalk. They were to walk beside each other, and Margaret was to hold her hand. The two girls went from the dormitory to the cafeteria with no problems. After breakfast, they were on their way to class.

Class started at 8 a.m. The teacher said, "My name is Miss Thomas! I am your kindergarten teacher. I would like for everyone to stand and tell the class your name." Each child stood and gave their names. Margaret wasn't shy at all. She was a big girl, now. She was in school to learn and meet new friends.

On Saturday morning, Carolyn didn't come as usual. Margaret sat on the side of her bed. 12 roommates shared her bedroom. She listened for the other girls but she didn't hear anyone. "Where is everybody?" she thought. No one said a word. She made her way to the window and turned her head to listen for voices. She heard children playing, but, what about her? Tears ran down her cheeks. It finally hit her.

"Momma! Daddy!" she cried. She tapped on the window, but no one heard her. Then suddenly, she heard footsteps coming towards her door. She reached out her hands to go open the door. It was Miss Haywood. She walked in the room and asked, "What's wrong Margaret?" She dried her eyes and said, "I thought everyone had left me here by myself! I want my momma. I want to go home." Miss Haywood tried to console her. She told Margaret that her parents were a long way from her, but she could call them. Margaret told her to call her momma, and she didn't want to stay any longer. It was time for her to go home. Miss Haywood took Margaret to her office. "You can talk to your grandmother, but you must understand, you cannot go home today. This is your school, now! You can only go during the holidays. The next holiday will be Thanksgiving. Do you understand, Margaret?"

Miss Haywood dialed the number to Hattie's home. "Mrs. Hailey. This is Miss Haywood at the school for the blind. I have Margaret here. She wants to talk to you. Please assure her that she will be okay, and you will see her the day before Thanksgiving."

Miss Haywood gave Margaret the phone. "Hey, Momma!" she cried. "I want to come home. I miss you and Daddy. Yes, Ma'am. Yes. Okay!" Margaret gave the phone to Miss Haywood. Hattie wanted to speak to her. "Miss Haywood, Margaret seems upset. I tried to make her feel better by telling her she had to stay until we get money for gas, but we are coming next Saturday to see my baby. Please don't tell her we are coming. I want it to be a surprise." Miss Haywood agreed to keep Hattie's secret. Margaret felt better and wanted to go outside with her roommates to play.

The following weekend, Lexie and

Hattie were back on the road to Raleigh. Once again, Lexie had to ride in the front seat. He had to have his favorite snacks, pound cake and a soda. They arrived at noon again. Hattie didn't see Margaret on the playground. She walked to her dormitory and asked for Miss Haywood. As she was about to open the door, Miss Haywood met her. "Hello, Mrs. Hailey. I see that you made it!

Margaret did better this week. I think she just wanted to hear your voice. I'm going to walk to the playground with you. She's out there somewhere!" she said.

Hattie looked across the field to see if she saw Margaret. All the children looked the same to her. "There she is!" yelled Miss Haywood. The two women walked to the merry-go-round and saw Margaret on a horse with one of her friends. Miss Haywood called Carolyn. "When the ride stops, walk Margaret over here. Her parents are here to see her."

When the ride stopped, Margaret and Carolyn ran across the field. "Is that my momma?" cried Margaret. Hattie met her baby halfway across the field. She grabbed Margaret and held her tightly in her arms. "Momma, I missed you. I wanted you to come back for me, but you can go back now! I'll be alright. I'm having fun. I'll be ready for Thanksgiving. I promise! I won't cry anymore!" Hattie looked at Miss Haywood and smiled and said, "We're going back home. Call me if you need too!"

When Hattie got in the car, she told her son that everything was alright, and it was time to go home. Lexie didn't argue about the gas. He wanted to go to Raleigh for the ride and the snacks. The Hailey's took their time driving back home. They had a hard time getting money for gas the first time, but Lexie was happy to buy gas on this trip, it was only $.25 a gallon this week.

...

November 1955

The Hailey family was preparing for the holidays. There was a new vinyl rug for the kitchen, and new curtains for the living room. The trip to Raleigh was coming up in a few more weeks. "Ah, what, what day are we, ah going to Raleigh?" asked Lexie. Hattie looked at the calendar and told him it would be the following Wednesday. She wanted to travel early in the mornings so she could be back home before dark.

It was the day before Thanksgiving and the car was filled with gas and looked like a shiny new nickel! Their son Ray knew how to keep a car clean! He wasn't going anywhere before he washed his car.

It was another long trip up Highway 1 North. Lexie was in his favorite seat, looking out the window and helping to drive. They stopped at the same service station and bought snacks. Hattie stopped at the same store in Sanford, to use the bathroom.

Finally, the sign on the highway read, "Garner, North Carolina, 30 miles." Everyone was excited about seeing Margaret and talking to her house mother. They wanted to know how she was adapting to her new home. Did she cry to go home? Was she learning like the other children? Hattie was ready for answers. If needed to, she was willing to take Margaret back and teach her at home.

Soon they reached their destination. Everyone got out to stretch their legs. They didn't see the children at the playground. Hattie looked around the campus. She walked to the building where Margaret stayed. Miss Haywood spotted Hattie from the window in her office. She walked outside and waved her hand to get Hattie's attention. "Mrs. Hailey, come this way! Margaret is in her room with the other girls."

Hattie walked to the entrance door and met Miss Haywood. The two women greeted each other and went to Margaret's room. As Miss Haywood opened the door, Margaret was sitting on her bed studying the 575 braille words she had to learn for first grade vocabulary. She was having fun learning with the other children. Hattie looked at her baby and tears flowed down her face. She took a handkerchief out of her coat pocket and wiped her eyes. Miss Haywood watched as Hattie stood there. "Margaret," called Miss Haywood! "Your grandmother is here!" Margaret turned her head to sense her grandmother. "Momma, you're here to get me?" she asked.

Hattie walked over to the bed, picked her baby up in her arms, and asked, "Are you having fun with your classmates?" Margaret gave her grandmother a great big hug and said, "I'm ready to go, but can I come back after Thanksgiving?" Miss Haywood looked at Hattie and gave her "thumbs up" for a job well done.

When Hattie got to the car, Lexie got out to give Margaret a hug, and said, "Ah, look at you big girl! Ah, we, ah, we missed you. You, ah, you have gotten taller since, ah, since the last time." He opened the back door of the car. Hattie and Margaret got in, and Ray drove to the highway and headed home.

Thanksgiving Day

Everyone was up early Thanksgiving morning. Hattie was preparing a feast for her family. She was expecting all her children (except for Effie) and their families to come. Lucius was the only son who had three children and one on the way. Effie called to speak to her baby girl and wished everyone a happy Thanksgiving. The boys in the family were dating, but didn't want to invite anyone for dinner, so Hattie invited her Aunt Ollie and her sister Della instead.

The table was set with a fancy white tablecloth. The blue Dutch pattern dishes were set with Hattie's' finest silverware. The guests sat in the living room with Margaret. She carried on conversations with her uncles like a big girl. She played with her first cousins, Pete, Irene, and Evangeline.

It was almost time to say the blessing. Lexie took his special seat at the head of the table. Hattie asked all the family to come into the dining room. The Lord had been good to the Haileys. He spared their first granddaughter, kept the family safe on the dangerous highway, and blessed them to have an increase in the family. Hattie wanted to thank Him for everything that had happened to them. Lexie looked at Hattie and told her to say it! She looked at him out of the corner of her eyes and said, "Do you want to say the blessing, Lexie?"

He didn't say a word. His eyes were shut tight, and his hand was on his coffee jar.

Hattie asked everyone to bow their heads, and she prayed a powerful Thanksgiving prayer: "Lord, the Lord of all Your people. We come this evening gathered in Your majestic name. We come with our eyes closed and our minds on You. We have so much to be thankful for, God. But, if we all had 10,000 tongues, it wouldn't be enough to show how grateful we are. You took care of my momma and daddy years ago, and I know in my heart, You are going to take care of this family. Thank You, Lord for health and strength. Thank You for another Thanksgiving Day. Thank You for my family, my relatives, the food we are about to receive. Thank You for saving our souls and most of all for dying for us all. In Jesus name I pray. Let everyone say, 'Amen.'" When Lucius opened his eyes, he saw his dad sipping coffee from his jar. He looked at him and shook his head.

Everyone enjoyed the dinner and afterward, they sang hymns while one of the children played the piano. The grandchildren played in the front bed-room and the grownups gathered around the piano singing, "How I Got Over!"

...

The family rose early Sunday morn-ing to take Margaret back to Raleigh. Hattie packed Margaret's clothes and made sandwiches and KoolAid for a snack. Margaret was ready to go. She missed her friends at school, and she wanted to learn more about her classes. She was told by her house mother that when the next semester started after Christmas, she would learn to read books. That was her conversation with her grand-mother on their long trip back to school.

Hattie was tired and laid her head back to get a nap. Margaret touched her grandma's hands, then her arms, and finally, her face to see if her eyes were closed. She moved Hattie's purse and laid her head on her lap. Everyone was asleep, except Lexie and the driver. Lexie looked at Ray and said, "Don't forget to stop at, at, that, ah, store so I, I can, can get me ah, a cake and a drink!" Ray didn't say a word. He pulled off the highway and stopped at the store. Hattie and Margaret were still fast asleep. When they arrived at the school, Hattie held Margaret's hand and walked to the dormitory. Margaret led the way. She couldn't wait to get back to her friends, the playground, and the teachers in her class.

Christmas 1955

It would be a wonderful Christmas this year. Effie was coming home and would be bringing her family with her. She wanted to see her little daughter. Hattie would tell her how she was doing in school, but she wanted to put her hands on her and see for herself.

She and George went shopping for the children. They bought Margaret a beautiful doll that stood three feet tall, a tea set that was made from real metal, and a cooking set, too. She had a spinning top, clothes, shoes, and always chose a hat to match each outfit. She wanted her daughter to be the prettiest little girl in Wadesboro.

Hattie was looking for Effie on Christmas Eve. The weather was pleasant. There was no snow or rain in the forecast. It was just sunny and a little chilly.

Around noon, a car pulled up in the driveway. It was George, Effie and the family. He got out and opened the door for Effie. Lexie was sitting on the front porch. He looked through the bushes to see who it was. "Light, and, ah, ah, come on in the house." Effie got out the car and walked to the front porch and yelled, "Hi Daddy!" She grabbed him around his neck and gave him her baby. George opened the trunk of the car and got their bags. "Y'all come on in the house, here!" said Lexie. Hattie came to the front room to see what all the commotion was about. She took Margaret by the hand and walked to the porch, and yelled, "Hey, my girl. Come on in the house!" Effie hugged her mom and reached down to greet her baby girl. She picked her up in her arms and kissed her on her cheeks. She began stroking her curly locks of hair and feeling her all over. "Hey, my big girl!" She carried Margaret in the house and sat on the sofa. Margaret smiled and touched her mom's face. She didn't speak, she just laid on her shoulder and smiled. Effie looked over her arm and said, "How is school and your new friends and teachers?" Margaret smiled with excitement. She talked about her friends and her teachers. She talked about the playground and the merry-go-round nonstop. The two were inseparable! All around the house, Effie held on to her daughter's hand.

Later that night, Margaret and Effie talked about Santa Claus. She asked Margaret what she wanted Santa to bring her. Margaret smiled and said, "I want a baby doll and a tea set and a tricycle. And some fruit and nuts and candy!" Effie sat on the bed listening to Margaret. "Well, I hear you have been a good little girl and we are going to make sure you get just what you want," she said while holding her little hands.

...

Margaret woke her mother and grandmother at 5 a.m. She said she wanted to go to the bathroom. Effie got up and took her to the toilet. On their way back to bed, Margaret walked slowly and turned her head and wigged her nose as if she smelled something. "I smell candy and fruit!" she said. She stopped and turned to the scent that smelled so good! Effie looked at her, and said, "Wait a minute! I think Santa has been here. Oh, my! I see a beautiful doll near the tree!" Margaret stopped in her tracks. She held her arms out to go in the direction of the tree. When she got there, she knelt to the floor. Just in front of the tree stood a doll as tall as she! She touched the doll's hair, her dress, and then her shoes and legs. She reached a little further under the tree and found the tea set. She stood up and moved on the other side of the tree, and there it was! She reached her hands out and felt the handlebars on her new red and white tricycle. She began to shake all over! Her feet started dancing excitedly. She was so happy she wanted to scream, but she was afraid her granddaddy would wake up and come out yelling, "Stop that, ah, that fuss!"

Margaret was thrilled. She got everything she wanted for Christmas and more! Then, she heard a soft knock on the front door. It was her cousin Pete, his little sister, and their dad. The children gathered around the tree and discussed what Santa had bought them for Christmas.

After a few days, Effie and George were packing their bags to leave for Jersey. They had a long talk with Margaret about school and told her to continue to do well in her classes. Hattie packed a bag of food for the family to take on their trip. "Don't forget to go by your mother's, George, and give her my love!" she said, before they drove off.

Chapter 6

. . .

School was out for the summer. The trip was always the same, but this time a surprise was going also. Hattie asked Lucius if Irene could ride with them. "Margaret needs someone to talk to on those long trips. I want to surprise her this time. We won't tell her until we get to the school," she explained to Lucius. He and his wife agreed to let her go.

Irene was so excited about going across the long bridge that she heard Margaret talk about. Lucius carried Irene in his arms to his mom's house. Everyone was standing in the living room ready to load the car. Lucius walked in the house and said, "Y'all take care of my baby and drive safe!" They greeted him and Hattie held on to Irene's hand.

They left the house around 6 a.m. About 30 minutes later, Irene stood up

97

and put her forehead to the window to see the river. She grabbed her grandma's hand and closed her eyes. "What's wrong baby?" asked Hattie. Irene held tight and asked, "Are we going across the bridge, yet?" Her grandma knew what was going on with her. She was afraid of the bridge! "Come close to me, Baby! We're almost across the water. It's okay! We're not going to fall in!" Hattie said, as she smiled holding her granddaughter tightly.

They arrived at Garner by noon. Everyone got out the car. They needed to stretch their legs and Irene had to use the bathroom for the fifth time. As they were getting back in the car, Hattie told her to stay with her granddad until she got back. "Where are you going?" cried Irene. Hattie didn't speak. She walked as fast as she could to Margaret's dormitory.

Soon, Hattie came walking across the lawn holding Margaret's hand and bags. "Margaret!" yelled Irene. "Ah, shut, shut, your mouth, girl! Sit back and be quiet!" her granddad, scolded. Irene was very anxious to see Margaret.

She jumped up and down in her seat, as Margaret got closer to the car. She wanted to laugh, but she put her hands over her mouth to keep from letting her laugh out. Hattie opened the trunk of the car to put the bags in. She opened the back door of the car and Margaret stopped. She turned her head to the right side, then the left side. She felt the seat and yelled, "Irene! Is that you?" Irene couldn't hold it any longer. "This is me!" she said.

Margaret got in the car, and she sat down next to her favorite little cousin. The girls hugged and laughed and hugged some more! Margaret was so happy to have someone else to talk to and play games with. The ride back home didn't seem so long this time.

...

There would only be a few weeks of summer vacation. Effie was coming on the 4th of July and would bring her family. Hattie wanted to see her other grandchildren for the summer, too.

She and Lexie had five grands now.

A homemade swimming pool was placed in the back yard for the girls. Alex, Lexie, and Hattie's baby boy filled the big tin tub with water. Effie ordered a swing set and had the store to deliver it to the house for Margaret. The Christmas gifts were strewn all over the lawn, including the red and white tricycle. No need for a swimming suit: all the kids took off their clothes and wore their under clothes to play in. Lexie sat on the high back porch and watched the children play. "Ah, don't, don't, y'all throw that, ah, that water, in her eyes!" Margaret didn't care about getting water in her eyes. She was happy to have her cousins with her for the summer.

First Grade at The State School for the Blind and Deaf

Margaret was more eager to learn this year than ever before. She was going to the first grade. There was a new teacher and new subjects to conquer. Reading was her favorite subject.

Miss Mozell Jones welcomed her class to the learning lab. Their first book was, "Day in, Day Out." Margaret enjoyed her classmates and excelled in reading. She knew all her braille words. She learned new words as well.

In the next semester of first grade, she learned to write on a slate. Writing in braille gave her an opportunity to communicate with other people in her school. She wrote notes to teachers, her house mother, the housekeepers, and the principal. She enjoyed reading and writing so much, that she decided to go to the school's Library and research for books of other subjects. She wanted to learn more about the world.

The Thanksgiving and Christmas holidays were the same for the Hailey family. Effie came home with her family and Lexie and Hattie made the trip back to Raleigh again.

The year flew by and Margaret was ready for her summer break. She missed her cousins and the little girl next door. Her name was Gail. She was the same age as Margaret. Her family moved from Washington, D.C. to her grandfather's house on Maple Lane Street. She was their only child, so having a friend next door was fun and exciting.

Margaret learned to dial the telephone. She would call Gail on the phone and ask her parents if she could come out to play. The girls would talk on the phone and make plans to meet at the fence. They would sit on the ground near the fence and talk to each other for hours. The only thing that separated them was evening, when it was time for dinner and getting ready for bed.

Three Months Later

It was time for another school year. Hattie called Effie to let her know that Margaret had outgrown most of her school clothes. "Momma, I will send a box next week for Margaret. She is growing like a weed this year. Let me know if she needs anything else," she said.

The box came on time for their

Raleigh trip. The family got up early and was waiting on Ray. He had to wipe the car clean while the dew was still on the freshly waxed coat.

They arrived on campus at 1 p.m. Margaret got out of the car first, followed by her grandmother. Going to the dormitory wasn't so hard to do, this time. The students who were in the fourth grade met Margaret at the entrance door. Freddie and Geraldine heard the children call Margaret's name. They stopped to speak to her. "Hello Margaret!" Freddie reached out to touch Margaret's head, and said, "My, you have gotten taller this year. Do you remember Geraldine, my friend? She's here with me." Geraldine reached out to touch Margaret's hand and greeted her too. "We're going to come back on the weekend and stay with you awhile!" said Freddie.

Miss Haywood was on the hall greeting new parents and students. "Hello, Margaret and Mrs. Hailey. I want to introduce you to Margaret's second grade teacher, Miss Thorpe! She will take you to the second grade hall."

Hattie greeted Miss Thorpe and introduced Margaret. Miss Thorpe walked them to her classroom. She explained to Hattie the subjects Margaret would be taking during the year. "Margaret will learn to play the piano this year. Her teacher will be Miss Davis. She will also have a class in Music Appreciation with Miss Robinson. I will be teaching her English, Spelling, Arithmetic and Science. She also has a new book this semester, "Down the River Road.""

School would be different this year. The children were placed in groups—A group and B group. Playtime included tricycles and sandboxes. Ring games and story time took place after lunch and nap time. All students learned to sing the blessing before each meal.

Margaret sat quietly beside her grandmother. She listened carefully. She held her grandma's hand and touched the side of her shoe. She didn't want to rush the women, but it was time for her family to get on the road to go home. She heard the children playing on the merry-go-round, and she wanted to have time to play too.

...

Margaret was now halfway through second grade. The Thanksgiving Day and Christmas holidays were over. It was time for Margaret to take piano lessons again. Her teacher decided that she was no longer a beginner in her class. She talked to Margaret about going to an advanced classes for piano lessons. "Margaret, your teacher for this semester will be Miss Davis, again. She teaches all the advanced students. You have really excelled this year. Do you have a piano at home?" she asked Margaret as they walked down the hallway to meet Miss Davis.

Margaret had no problems learning to play the piano. She played as if she was born to play. Reading her book was easy for her to do. She knew all her spelling words in braille too.

School Days

After the second grade, she went through third grade learning with Miss Johnson. Her fourth grade teacher was Miss Mann. Miss Housen was her Home Economics teacher. In fifth grade, her homeroom teacher was Mr. Malone and Miss Logan taught her typing.

In sixth grade, Margaret wanted to join the band. Mr. Edwards was the band's director and knew how well Margaret loved instruments. The flute was another favorite instrument she wanted to play, and she was successful with that instrument. She played so well that she was seated first in that class!

Margaret's seventh grade homeroom teacher was Mrs. Boykin, and her classes were getting easier each year. She excelled in school.

The school board decided to change the name of the school this year. All the students had to go to the auditorium for a meeting with the staff. Mr. Crockett announced that the new name for the school would be "Governor Morehead School." Everyone stood and clapped for the excellent work the staff and the school board had done.

Finally, it was time for junior high classes. Mr. Stokes was Margaret's eighth grade homeroom teacher. She wanted to join the school's Glee Club in the eighth grade but had to wait until the following year. Miss Robinson was the director for the Glee Club. Margaret enjoyed singing with her classmates and the older students at her school. In her tenth grade year, Mr. Stokes had the privilege of teaching Margaret again.

The same week, Margaret inquired about a young girl name Freddie. "Mr. Crockett, do you know a girl that goes to this school by the name, Freddie?" she asked. He told her that he did, and she had a friend named Geraldine. "I know those girls very well. They are two of the smartest students that have ever gone to this school. Do you know them, Margaret?" he asked. Margaret smiled at him and said, "Yes, I do! Freddie is from my hometown. I don't know where Geraldine is from!" Mr. Crockett told Margaret that the girls were attending college, now. "Those girls graduated with honors, and both got accepted at the college of their choice. I'm going to do my best to keep in touch with their future. I know they will be successful," he added.

Now, it was time for Margaret to enter high school. 11th grade was a challenge! Mr. Harris was a hard, but he was a great teacher. He was preparing Margaret for college. He knew how hard she worked in elementary and middle school. He wanted her to succeed in high school too.

Now, Margaret was in the twelfth grade. Her teacher, Mrs. Crockett (who was also the senior class advisor) said, "Margaret, since you are a senior this year, I suggest you take French 2. It will look great on your transcript and resume. Mrs. Freeman is our foreign language teacher. I have audited your classes for this semester." Margaret agreed. She thanked Mrs. Crockett for all her suggestions to help her be more successful in school and to prepare for college.

Class of 1968

Letters were sent out to the families of each senior. Hattie received a letter from the school about Margaret's graduation and her accomplishments. The Hailey family was proud of their granddaughter. A letter was sent to Effie and her family too. She wasn't going to miss the moment her daughter marched to receive her diploma.

The family prepared for their trip to Raleigh. The boys were getting older and were dating now. They were thankful to God for allowing them safe and blessed trips for all those years. "Ah, is this, ah, our last time going, ah, going to Raleigh?" asked Lexie. Hattie didn't say a word, she just gave him a look. "Yes Daddy, this will be the last trip to the blind and deaf school," said their son, Ray. Lexie was sitting at the dining room table sipping his coffee. He laughed loudly and said, "Ah, I'm going, to miss, going on that, ah, long country road. The polices didn't, ah, stop us, not one, ah, one time in all, all, those years. White folks, ah, can be, ah, good, ah, when they, ah, want too!" Hattie stopped what she was doing and smiled at her husband. She thought he would say something about the money he spent buying all those pound cakes and sodas for 13 years, but he didn't.

The car was cleaned, and the trunk was empty. They had to leave room for all of Margaret's clothes and books.

The trip seemed shorter this time. A new highway was built, and they didn't have to go through all the small towns. They arrived at 8 a.m.

The graduation ceremony would start at 9 a.m. in the school's auditorium.

Everyone got out of their cars and went to the bathrooms on campus. They looked for Margaret, but she was waiting in another area of the school. The Hailey family walked in the crowded Auditorium. They found seats near the front of the building.

Music was playing as the graduates lined up on both sides of the building. When the Hailey family saw Margaret marching with her class, they began clapping for her. When all the graduates were seated, everyone waited patiently for the commencement to start.

The program started with someone saying the prayer. When Effie looked at her program, she saw Margaret's name listed as Salutatorian. Effie nudged her mother's arm, and said, "Look Momma. Someone is taking Margaret to the podium! She is going to give the welcome for her class!" Hattie raised up in her seat and looked at Effie. Tears of pride flowed down their faces. When Margaret got to the podium, she opened her mouth and spoke well. She pronounced each word with authority. Everyone on stage stopped and stared. "That's my baby up there!" Effie grabbed her mom's hand, and said, "Thank you, Momma!" Hattie looked at her and said, "No, you thank God! He has her on display today! She is displaying the mighty works of our Heavenly Father."

The class of 1968 stood as their

names were called. When Margaret stood up to receive her high school diploma, all the family members stood also. They were happy to see their daughter graduate from high school. Hattie looked over her shoulder, thinking that she heard someone crying. It was her husband wiping his eyes. He was sad and happy at the same time.

When graduation was over, the family went to the area where the seniors gathered. When they arrived, Margaret was surrounded by her classmates. They all hugged each other and said how they were going to miss the school.

Effie spotted Margaret and told the family to follow her. "Oh, my beautiful daughter, you did an outstanding job on stage," she said, as she hugged and kissed Margaret. "I wasn't nervous until the Marshall came to get me," she said. The students continued to congratulate each other. There was a young man standing near Margaret. She was holding on to his hand. "Momma, this is Joseph Faison. He's my boyfriend! He was in the band with me. We have been dating since the 11th grade. Joseph, this is my mother, Effie and my grandma, Mrs. Hattie Hailey!" The young man spoke to her parents and continued to express his feelings for Margaret. Effie talked with the young man and wished him well in the future. "I pray that you continue your education and become the man God wants you to be. Please stay in touch with Margaret and the family," she said. Soon everyone said goodbye and went their separate ways.

Chapter 7

. . .

June 1968

Margaret received a letter from Western Carolina University, in Cullowhee, North Carolina. She would be there for 6 weeks. This school would prepare her for the four years she would spend at Shaw University in Raleigh, North Carolina.

. . .

The Greyhound bus was parked on Maple Lane Street to assist Margaret to her destination. The driver got off the bus to load her luggage. "Hello, Miss Hailey. I see we are meeting again. Where are you going this time?" he asked. "I'm going to Western Carolina University in Cullowhee. It's in the mountains. Do you know about that city?" she asked. The driver assured her that he was very familiar with WCU.

Margaret was a fighter for success. She was ready to explore, to challenge herself, and work hard in the classroom. She would be inspired by a community of supporters that recognized her potentials and were willing to help define and achieve her goals in life. WCU had great teachers and mentors. Margaret was looking forward to learning all she could and to become another successful black woman from Wadesboro, North Carolina.

When her time at WCU was over, Margaret was back home for the summer. The mailman was delivering the mail at his usual time. Margaret heard the mail truck park in front of the house. She opened the door, and the mailman came to the door and said, "Hello. I have a letter from WCU for Miss Margaret Marie Hailey. Here's your other mail also!" Margaret thanked him and walked back in the house. To her surprise, the letter was in braille. She opened it and started reading. It informed Margaret that she had earned B's in all of her courses. She was so happy. She called her grandma and told her the good news. "I knew you could do it, baby. You have always been a smart girl!" said Hattie.

Margaret decided to go visit her mother before going to Shaw. She wanted to spend time with her other siblings. She knew that New Jersey was a big place, and she would be faced with many challenges there. Effie lived in a two-story house in Camden. Hattie's house didn't have stairs. She was the only child in her grandparents' house, while Effie had four children and one on the way.

Camden, New Jersey

Effie met Margaret at the bus terminal. They rode on the streetcar to Effie's house. When they arrived, all the children were waiting to see their oldest sister. Everyone wanted to help Margaret do something. One grabbed her bag; another one helped her to the sofa and the girls wanted to play. It was too much for this country girl!

She stayed for a week and wanted to go back home. "Momma, I think I should leave on Monday. Orientation at Shaw University is next Wednesday." Her mother didn't try to change her mind. "Okay, I will get the bus fare and your ticket the first thing in the morning!" Effie wanted her daughter to stay longer, but she understood. Margaret was a grown woman now. She was the only little girl at her grandparent's house. Her siblings wanted to help Margaret because she was blind. But she wasn't helpless! Effie had to put her own feelings aside and think about Margaret.

Effie took Margaret to the bus terminal. When they arrived, she wanted to explain to the driver that her daughter was blind and needed assistance. "Mother, you don't have to explain to him that I'm blind. He knows that I have a disability. I will be okay. I'll call you when I get home. I love you! Please don't worry about me. God has been with me all these years. He's not going to leave me now!" Effie smiled and kissed Margaret on the cheek. As she stepped off the bus, she stopped and said, "I love you, and be careful! Tell everyone I said, hello!"

Margaret was back in Wadesboro at

11:30 p.m. Lexie and Hattie were up waiting for the bus to park in the road. "Ah, Hattie, Hattie Mae, ah, go, go to the door. The ah, bus, is, ah out there," said Lexie happily. Hattie saw the bus before he did, but she didn't say a word. She went to the front door and turned the outside light on. "Here I am!" she called to the driver. Margaret was getting off the bus with no assistance. This wasn't her first time riding the bus. Hattie walked to the road and reached for Margaret's bag. "I got it Momma! Just let me hold your arm!" she said.

September 1968

Summer vacation was now over. Shaw University's orientation would start the first Wednesday in September.

The Hailey family packed all of Margaret's clothes for the fall semester. They were excited that she would go to college. But Hattie decided not to travel this time. The boys could help Margaret with all her luggage and books. Lexie had no desire to travel that far anymore. He had retired from his part-time job, and his only enjoyment now was watching the wrestling programs on television with his next-door neighbor.

"You all be careful on the highway! Here's a packed lunch for you to enjoy on your way. Margaret, you let them know when you need to use the bathroom!" said Hattie. Margaret didn't argue with her grandma. She had always been very protective of her, and it wasn't going to change now. "Bye Momma, we will call you when we get there. I love you and Daddy," she said, as they drove away.

Shaw University, Raleigh, North Carolina

Margaret arrived at Shaw in time for Orientation, which began at 10 a.m. One of the students helped Margaret to sign in and gave her an information packet.

While she was standing in line, she heard a familiar voice. She turned her head and asked, "Is that you Evonne?" The young lady stepped out of line and said, "Margaret! Margaret Hailey is that you?"

When Margaret received her packet, she stepped out of line, and there was Evonne standing nearby. The two girls greeted each other and began to talk about coming to Shaw. "Do you remember Connie?" she asked Margaret. Connie stood near one of the tables. She heard someone call her name. "Did someone call Connie? If so, I'm here!" The three girls stepped aside and began talking about old times at their school in Garner. "I'm thankful that we are here together. We can say we know someone at this school!" one of the girls said.

...

Margaret was given her schedule for the first semester. Most of her classes were elective classes. English was no problem for her. It was one of her favorite subjects. She also had math, home economics, and fine arts. She earned all A's during her first semester. In her dormitory, Connie and Evonne shared bedrooms with her on the fifth floor of their building. Going out on the town to party wasn't something

Margaret enjoyed, so she spent her leisure time studying or reading her favorite books.

When the first semester ended, Margaret went back to Wadesboro to visit her parents and friends.

December 1968

Margaret decided to go see Effie again in New Jersey. She stayed there for two weeks and then it was back to Wadesboro before going to Shaw.

When she arrived back from New Jersey, her friend Edna was standing in her front door, watching for the bus to park. She walked to the road and waited for Margaret to get off. "Hey, girl! You sure keep the road busy!" she said as she offered to help Margaret off the bus. "I'm so glad to get home. That was a long ride, and I had to change buses two times!" said Margaret, as she handed Edna her bags.

The two girls walked inside the house and greeted Hattie and Lexie. "Momma, I'm so glad to be home. Is Daddy doing okay?" she asked. Hattie didn't want to say too much about Lexie's health condition. She didn't want Margaret to worry. She knew that she had enough on her plate with going to school and getting familiar with her classes. "Your granddaddy is doing alright. He is hard-headed and won't do like the doctor told him. We all are in God's hands! How did you enjoy your trip to Jersey?" she asked, as Margaret unpacked. "The girls and boys are getting older and doing well in school. Momma and George are busy working, so I decided to make my trip short," said Margaret.

Edna had a new "True Story" magazine. Those two girls loved reading love stories and fantasizing about the characters and their love lives. They went outside on the front porch and sat in the gliding swing. Edna read out loud. You could hear them laughing and talking about the book all the way to Lexie's room. They made sure not to disturb her granddaddy, Lexie. He would put a stop to all the giggling.

Weeks passed. Margaret was ready to go back to Raleigh. Edna had a job and was ready to go back to school, also.

Sophomore Year at Shaw University

Margaret's third year at Shaw went by quickly. She had more classes that year, and she stayed in her books. At the end of that year, she made one B and four A's. Her parents were proud of her. They encouraged her to continue to do well in school. If she needed anything, she could always call home. They were willing to do without for their granddaughter. Hattie always believed that God would make a way for Margaret. She never pitied her granddaughter. God had a plan for her just like He had a plan for the children that could see.

Hattie loved to read the Book of Psalms in the Bible. One of her favorites was, *"You made all the delicate, inner parts of my body and knit me together in my mother's womb. Thank You Lord! Your workmanship is marvelous, how well I know it." (Psalm 139:13, 14)*

Junior Year at Shaw University

Margaret was studying in her major

this year. Her classes were getting harder, so she had to stay focused and continued to do her best. She always wanted to be a Social Worker. She enjoyed people. She wanted to help them to become better citizens. She loved giving good advice, learning their personalities, and what made them think the way they did. Everything about a person was interesting to her.

The following year, she had to do her internship in Anson and Union Counties. She received a letter from the school stating that someone from Anson County Social Services, would pick her up at 8 a.m. She worked with Anson County social workers on Mondays, Tuesdays, and Wednesdays. On Thursdays and Fridays, she was in Union County.

Senior Year at Shaw University

Margaret was on display again for the Lord. She knew without a doubt that the Lord would be with her all the way through school. She read the Word of God just as she read and studied for school.

Although she couldn't see with her natural eyes, God was visible in her heart. She loved to read her Bible. *"Meditate on it day and night so you will be sure to obey everything written in it. Only then will you prosper and succeed in all you do. This is my command—be strong and courageous! Do not be afraid or discouraged. For the Lord your God is with you wherever you go." (Joshua 1:7).*

April 1972

Margaret graduated from Shaw University, receiving a B.A Degree in Sociology. Everyone was proud of her. She did it! It wasn't easy for her mother to leave her when she was a baby. It wasn't easy for Lexie and Hattie to save money to go back and forth to Raleigh all those years, and it wasn't easy for Margaret to study in a classroom with sighted students. Some cared about her disability, and some didn't! God never left her. She was praying when others were doubting.

After graduation, Margaret went back

to Wadesboro. She wanted to stay with her grandparents until Mother's Day. Her granddaddy wasn't doing well. He was in and out of the hospital. Hattie prayed day and night for her husband. Margaret could sense that something was wrong. "Daddy isn't talking much, and Momma won't tell me everything that's going on!" she thought. She heard Hattie talking to Lexie, "You need to eat something. Just sip a little of this soup!" said Hattie. But Margaret didn't hear Lexie respond. He wasn't talking at all. "That's not Daddy in there! He's supposed to argue with Momma or say something! He is getting old. I believe the Lord is coming to get my daddy," she thought. Lexie was in bed for several weeks. It was time for him to go get medical help.

Hattie did all she could for her husband. All the soup, rubbing him down with alcohol, rubbing his head with mentholated rubs and praying, wasn't going to do Lexie any good. God would step in and take him home.

Hattie decided to call her children. She wanted to take Lexie to the hospital. "Boys, I have done all I can do for your daddy. Call the ambulance so he can see a doctor there." While the ambulance was on the way, Margaret sat quietly in her room with her Bible, and she read, *"How frail is humanity! How short is life, how full of trouble! We blossom like a flower and then wither. Like a passing shadow, we quickly disappear. Must you keep an eye on such a frail creature and demand an accounting from me? Who can bring purity out of an impure person? No one! You have decided the length of our lives, and we are not given a minute longer."* (Job 14:1-5).

"God's working again!" said Margaret, while sitting in her grandma's room. She waited silently until her granddaddy left the house for the last time.

Chapter 8

. . .

June 24, 1972

The news of Lexie Dennis Hailey's passing spread quickly all over Coley Hill. He was a good neighbor, and a hard-working man. Hattie would miss her husband. The house would be different without him trying to listen to his television programs and trying to hear the neighborhood gossip at the same time.

May 1973

Margaret stayed with her grandma for about a year. She had a job interview in Washington, D.C. Lexie had a nephew in D.C. who had four daughters. They were nurses and worked at the county hospital there. She rode the Greyhound Bus to her cousin's house. When she arrived, she settled down for a day and then she applied for many jobs in that area. Some she liked and some she didn't.

Later that month, she decided to return to New Jersey. She applied at several Social Services and Human Services offices. She prayed and she waited on God.

September 1973

She decided to go back home. The bus was crowded, and it was hot. When she got to Maple Lane, the bus driver said, "See you in a few days, Miss Hailey!" She said goodbye and walked down the driveway and wondered about the driver's strange comment.

She walked in the house and put her things away. As she sat on the side of the bed she said to herself, "I'm just riding from place to place. I know God has something for me to do. He didn't bring me this far for nothing! Devil, you get out of my way!" She opened her Bible and found these words. *"Wait patiently for the Lord. Be brave and courageous. Yes, wait patiently for the Lord." (Psalm 27:14).*

She got up and found her grandma sitting at the dinner table. "Momma are you alright?" she asked. Hattie was sitting down reading her Bible and said, "You know Margaret, you are a blessing to this family. You are different from all our other grandchildren, and God made you that way. The Bible says, *'And we know that God causes everything to work together for the good of those who love Him and are called according to His purpose for them. (Roman 8:28).'*"

Hattie always knew that God had a special purpose for their first grandchild. He made her that way because He would get the glory. She thought about Lexie leaving them and knew her time was coming next. But there was no doubt in her heart that God would fulfill His promise. *"Do not be afraid or discouraged, for the Lord will personally go ahead of you. He will be with you; He will neither fail you nor abandon you. (Deuteronomy 31:8),"* she recited to Margaret.

September 1973

Margaret was home with her grandma when the phone rang. It was a social worker for the blind, in Greenville, North Carolina. They wanted to interview Margaret for a job. She would be responsible for three counties: Martin, Bertie, and Washington counties. The job would last for a year, with excellent pay. The bus driver was right! Margaret was on the road again.

She arrived in Greenville early Tuesday morning. The county supplied an apartment, transportation, a mentor, and a tour guide for her leisure time. She enjoyed talking to the young people and encouraging them to live better lives. Everyone praised her for a job well done.

Spring of 1975

She returned Wadesboro at the end of her assignment and worked for Amway. Business wasn't that great in that small town. She waited until the fall of that year and went back to the city she loved so dearly, Raleigh, North Carolina. There were several friends in the city who welcomed her to stay with them.

The Dixon family were good friends to Margaret. She had a job at the church where Reverend Dixon ministered. They were happy to see Margaret again. Reverend and Mrs. Dixon asked her to stay with them and play the piano and organ on Sundays. She accepted the offer. She was happy in Raleigh with her friends. She called her mother and her grandmother to tell them the wonderful news.

While she was in Raleigh, she met a man who worked for an agency for the blind. He offered her a job at his office. She was to evaluate employees for jobs and create different workshops for the agency. She accepted and did an outstanding job.

After a short time working there, she was recommended for another position with the federal government as a representative for the IRS. Margaret knew her God hadn't left her alone. Her administrator told her that she had to go to Arkansas for a three-week workshop. But she had to fly to get there!

Margaret couldn't help but think about her Heavenly Father. *"Everything He does reveals His Glory and Majesty. His righteousness never fails. She remembered all His wonderful works. How gracious and merciful is our God." (Psalm 111:3-4).*

During her stay in Arkansas, she completed her training, including her independent living classes.

December 1975

Back in North Carolina, Margaret was offered a job at the Center for the Blind in Butner. Her parents always encouraged her to focus on the good things in her life. No, she couldn't see, but she thanked God for good health and strength. She had a grateful attitude and was content no matter the circumstances. *"And this same God who takes care of me will supply all my needs from His glorious riches, which have been given to me in Christ Jesus." (Philippians 4:19).*

Margaret started her new job.

She typed her agenda for the week. She was there to encourage and give inspirational advice to young adults. There were students from all over the county.

One afternoon, a young man came to the office to talk with her. He was visually impaired but had some vision. He wanted to get information about several jobs that he saw posted in the lobby. "Excuse me, please!" he said, as he was passing her desk. "May I ask where you're from?" Margaret didn't address the young man. She gently asked him to get in line, and said, "Sir, I'm not here to answer your questions, I'm here to ask you questions. You will have to get in line, please." The man didn't get in line as she asked him to. He waited until everyone left the building so he could talk to Margaret alone.

The young man stood at Margaret's desk. She was typing her assignments for the next day. "Excuse me, Miss Hailey. May I call you Margaret?" he asked. She stopped what she was doing and closed her typewriter, and said, "Yes, you may." The young man cleared his throat. "I've been wanting to ask you something. Are you dating anyone?" he asked. Margaret was surprised. This man didn't know her, and she most definitely didn't know him.

She held her breath for a second and asked, "Why do you want to know?" He stood and looked around the lobby to see if anyone was standing near, and said, "I would love to take you out so we can get to know each other better. You are a beautiful lady!" Margaret was speechless. She was lonely for a relationship and needed to do more than just work all the time. She asked, "Aren't you blind, sir? How are you going to take me anywhere? The blind can't lead the blind, and that's the Word!" He grabbed a chair and sat next to Margaret and said, "Look, I'm a pretty good guy! I have friends and relatives that will take me anywhere I want to go. My sight is impaired! I can see things close up, but not far away. I see you, and you are beautiful, just like I said!"

Margaret then asked, "What is your name?" He leaned down to her and said, "Donnell Crudup!" Margaret and Donnell enjoyed each other's company. They went out to eat. They went to the theater and the fair. And then, they fell in love.

1976 – A New Life Begins

Donnell and Margaret decided to have a house wedding. The house was decorated in blue and silver. His parents made all the ribbons and corsages for the event. All the family members were there to wish them well. Margaret knew that her grandma couldn't come, but she sent invitations to her and Effie. They were happy for their daughter.

The next month, the newlyweds decided to move back to Raleigh. That was where they wanted to make their home. Donnell applied for an apartment, and they moved in shortly after. He was blessed to get a job at the Industry for the Blind, in Raleigh.

Margaret and Donnell were happy to be married. The married couple she had been around the most was her grandparents. She prayed for directions on how to be a good wife. One night, she opened her Bible and read, *"A man leaves his father and mother and is joined to his wife, and the two are united into one." (Genesis 2:24).* She wanted to know more, so she kept searching. *"Love does no wrong to others, so love fulfills the requirements of God's law." (Roman 13:10)*

Donnell and Margaret had their first child in 1977. He was a beautiful baby boy, whom they named Demetrius. She used all her training from her job to take care of her home and her baby. About a year later came another baby boy! He was born in 1978, and they named him Lamonte. Their hands were full! Donnell was working every day and Margaret was a stay-at-home mom.

Even when times were tough, Margaret didn't give up. She knew God was still on His throne. She stayed in the Word. As soon as the babies were asleep, she would open her Bible. *"Are any of you suffering hardship? You should pray. Are any of you happy? You should sing praises. Are any of you sick? You should call for the elders of the church to come and pray over you, anointing you with oil in the name of the Lord. Such a prayer offered in faith will heal the sick, and the Lord will make you well. And if you have committed any sins, you will be forgiven." (James 5:13-15).*

About a year and a half later, a new baby arrived. It was a girl and they named her Sonji.

Margaret continued to love and take care of her family, but it was hard work. The couple was getting to be overwhelmed by all the daily duties of being parents. The children were getting older. They were all in school. The meals had to be prepared by a certain time. Everything seemed to discourage Margaret. She was getting older, now.

Whenever she called home, the news was always the same. Her grandma was doing well, and her aunt Fannie had to move back home from New York. "I can't let living like this burden me down. Lord, You've got to show me the way!" She opened her Bible. *"Give your burdens to the Lord, and He will take care of you. He will not permit the godly to slip and fall." (Psalm 55:22).*

"For the Lord sees clearly what

a man does, examining every path he takes. An evil man is held captive by his own sins; they are ropes that catch and hold him. He will die for lack of self-control; he will be lost because of his great foolishness." (Proverbs 5:21-23).

Margaret and Donnell divorced. She had the responsibility of raising her children alone. But God was faithful, and He was still working behind the scenes.

Chapter 9

...

Summer of 1995

Now the Crudups were living in separate cities. The children were teenagers when Donnell decided to remarry. Margaret was in Durham, North Carolina. She lived with friends who loved her and offered her a room in their home. She was happy to be with friends who were God-fearing and didn't mind giving to others what God had given them.

One afternoon, she was sitting in her room reading a book. The phone rang. It was her mother, Effie, calling with bad news. Hattie had passed away. Margaret's heart was torn apart. The first thing that came to her mind was how her grandmother took care of her. She made sacrifices to take care of her grandchild. Margaret didn't want for anything.

When there was little money to buy food, Momma made a way to go get whatever she wanted. She always reminded her that just because she couldn't see with her physical eyes, there were grown people who could not see and had eyes. Her grandma always read the Bible to her and reminded her that God had her on display.

Margaret always thought of a display being on stage and everyone was clapping their hands for her. But that wasn't what she meant! Margaret would do many things in life because of her blindness. God would clear the paths for her. Whenever she fell, He would pick her up. He would provide for her. She would experience love, have children, go to college, fly in a plane, make the top scores in school, and have somewhere to live when the way seemed impossible. That's what her grandmother meant when she said Margaret would display the works of God. God did it, all by Himself.

Later. Margaret told her friends that her grandma had passed, and she would go to Wadesboro the following weekend.

Saturday Morning

Margaret got out of bed to answer the phone. To her surprise, it was her cousin, Pete. He wanted to know if she had transportation to come to their grandmother's funeral. She agreed to be ready by noon and started packing for the trip. Three hours later, Pete was at her apartment building. "Are you ready, Margaret?" he asked while entering her door. "I want you to stay overnight with me and my family. I will take care of you and bring you back tomorrow."

Hattie was laid to rest on Sunday. Everyone gathered at the home and enjoyed the food and read the sympathy cards. "Momma will be missed! I tried to make her happy in Jersey," said Effie.

Margaret sat quietly at the dining room table. She thought about her granddaddy sipping coffee out of his jar. She also thought about the good times she had with her cousins during the summer. "Do you remember Gail and Edna?" she asked her aunt. One of her uncles said he did, and told Margaret that they were still living—one in

Washington and the other one in Monroe.

Margaret was content. Life was like a cycle to her. Someone dies and someone is born, repeatedly.

"And now, dear brothers and sisters, we want you to know what will happen to the believers who have died so you will not grieve like people who have no hope. For since we believe that Jesus died and was raised to life again, we also believe that when Jesus returns, God will bring back with him the believers who have died. We tell you this directly from the Lord: We who are still living when the Lord returns will not meet him ahead of those who have died. For the Lord himself will come down from Heaven with a commanding shout, with the voice of the archangel, and with the trumpet call of God. First the Christians who have died will rise from their graves. Then, together with them, we who are still alive and remain in the Earth will be caught up in the clouds to meet the Lord in the air. Then we will be with the Lord forever. So, encourage each other with

these words." *(I Thessalonians 4:13-18).*

Margaret called Pete to let him know she was ready to go. She continued to think about the home she was leaving and loved so dearly. "Everything will be different, now!" she thought. She didn't have anyone else to call for spiritual advice anymore. She didn't know if this was her last time coming back to Wadesboro. She had children and that was enough hope for her. She prayed for them every day and night. She wasn't with them, but she knew who was—the same God that took care of her, was with them also. Nobody but God!

For many years, the disappointments and stresses of life were trying to get the best of Margaret. She was a fighter. She persevered! She was down for a while, but God always showed up at the right time.

"My thoughts are nothing like your thoughts," says the Lord. *"And my ways are far beyond anything you could imagine. For just as the Heavens are higher than the Earth, so my ways are higher than your ways and my thoughts higher than your thoughts." (Isaiah 55:8,9).*

Pete drove Margaret back to her home in Durham, N.C. They enjoyed talking about the good old days in Wadesboro. They laughed about their granddaddy Lexie and how he loved pound cakes and Pepsi Cola.

"God's been good to us all, Margaret. If it wasn't for Him, I don't know where me and my wife would be today. I thank Him all the time. We are getting closer to Durham, now, but we are going to keep you in our prayers," said Pete.

When they got to Margaret's house, Pete helped her to the door and unloaded all her bags in her bedroom, and said, "You be sweet and be good! I'll call you when we get back to Charlotte!" The two cousins hugged and said their good-byes.

Margaret lived in her apartment for many years. She had friends who met every need. Someone helped with cleaning the house; another helped with taking out the trash; and a close friend shopped for her groceries once a month. She was seldom alone. Someone was always coming by to see what she needed.

...

Many years passed before Margaret decided to move to another neighborhood. She was approved for a new apartment. She would be on her own again. "Look at God," she thought.

Friends helped her move and gave furniture for her new home. They were proud of her and were willing to do whatever she needed. She had someone to come in the home and do light chores. She later found out that one of her neighbors was from Wadesboro. They lived in the same building.

Margaret was sitting on her porch one day and heard someone call out to her and said, "Mrs. Hattie Mae Hailey! Mr. Lexie is your granddaddy! You are Margaret!" Margaret was surprised and answered back, "And who are you?" The lady walked up to Margaret and said her name was Carolyn. The two women talked for hours.

Carolyn offered to do whatever she could for Margaret. Whenever she received a letter from the family, Carolyn would offer to read it for her. She read all of Margaret's birthday cards, and Christmas cards. Margaret was thankful to have someone she knew at her apartment building.

"Hear me as I pray, O Lord. Be merciful and answer me! My heart has heard you say, 'Come and talk with me.' And my heart responds, Lord, I am coming. Do not turn your back on me. Do not reject your servant in anger. You have always been my helper. Don't leave me now; don't abandon me. O God of my salvation! Even if my mother and father abandon me, the Lord will hold me close." (Psalm 27:7-10).

Margaret lived in that apartment building for many years.

Year 2000

Margaret received a call from New Jersey. George had passed away. She hurt for her mom. Effie and George were married for many years. She was unable to go to his funeral but sent her condolences.

Things were looking better for Margaret. Her children visited her often.

She heard the sad news about her ex-husband's wife passing. She didn't hate him, but prayed for him. His wife's passing was devastating enough for him to bear.

•••

Margaret was getting older and needed more assistance. She had some bad days, and she didn't want to be a burden on anyone in her building. She started occupying herself with books. She read all the time. Every other week, the mailman had a load of books for her.

Chapter 10

. . .

May 2016

One day, Margaret was unable to get up on her own. Something happened to her legs. She called for someone to help her. The apartment manager called 911. The next day, Margaret was in the hospital.

"So, after you have suffered a little while, He will restore, support, and strengthen you, and He will place you on a firm foundation. All power to Him forever! Amen." (1 Peter 5:10).

She stayed in the hospital for three weeks. She had to have therapy to strengthen her legs. Finally, she was released and sent back home. Her body was weak, and she had to push herself to get up in the mornings. All kind of thoughts were going through her mind. "Am I going to get better? Will I lose my ability to walk?

What if I have to go to a rest home? What's going to happen to my things? Who will take care of my bills?" It was getting to be too much for one person to go through. She had to take control of her mind. "I'm not going anywhere until God says so." She made it to her table and got her Bible.

"So be strong and courageous! Do not be afraid and do not panic before them. For the Lord your God will personally go ahead of you. He will neither fail you nor abandon you." (Deuteronomy 31:6).

The recovery process was long. Margaret was getting better, but not to the point where she could be alone. She stayed at her apartment for another year. The health providers assisted her at home, and she did well.

One day she got an important phone call. It was her mother in New Jersey. "Hi, my girl! How are you doing in Durham?" she asked. Margaret didn't want to worry her and said she was fine. They stayed on the phone for a few minutes and discussed each other's challenges. "Yes, I'm having problems with my knees, but I just trust the Lord and keep going," Effie said. Margaret told her mother to take care of herself and she would do the same.

July 2017

Margaret had to go back to the hospital. She was getting weaker in her legs. She did not forget about God. She prayed and asked Him to provide!

May 2019

A call came from Camden, New Jersey. It was Margaret's sisters. "Mom isn't doing well this time. We will keep you informed," they said. Later that week, Effie passed away. Margaret's heart was broken. She loved her mother dearly. They didn't see each other often, but that distant love was strong. *"Never let love and faithfulness leave you! Tie them around your neck as a reminder. Write them deep within your heart."* (Proverbs 3:3).

Margaret was unable to go to her mother's funeral. She kept Effie in her heart as always. Many times, the story about the blind man would cross her mind. She read the story over and over for many years. Jesus saw this man who was blind from birth and was asked a question. "Why was this man born blind? Was it because of his parents' sins or his own sins?" It caused her to wonder about that! How could someone be born blind because of someone else's sin? Her mother didn't cause her blindness, and she never thought that it did. God had to be in control of the man's birth. He knitted him together in his mother's womb! She also liked the scripture that said, *"It was not because of his sins or his parents. He said this happened so the power of God could be seen." (John 9:1-3).*

Now that Effie was gone, she prayed that her mother didn't blame herself for Margaret's blindness. She could only imagine what was going through her mom's mind when she saw that her baby was blind. "I pray that my mother didn't leave this world thinking that she did something to cause me to be this way. As for my father, for many years I thought about him. I had questions I needed answers for, but I left it in God's hands. And in December 1988, I met my birth father for the first time. I didn't have to search for him. He came to see me.

I really haven't missed much in my life. I've never driven a car, but I heard of a blind man who did! Nothing is impossible with God! I married my husband and was engaged to another fellow before him! My boyfriend, John... Momma knew about him but didn't make much of it! Just a friend, she thought!

I've often thought about people running a red light and can see! Someone blind would have more sense than that! I'm blind, but there are people who can see a horse and are afraid to get on it! I got on a horse one time at Camp Dogwood for the Blind, and that horse took me for a ride of my life! There was no fear in this blind girl!

Some people can see the river and are afraid to ride down the stream, but not me! I got in a canoe, paddled a rowboat, and couldn't see where I was going, but I enjoyed it!

When I touch someone, I can't see the color of their skin. Everybody is the same color to me. But this is one thing I will never understand. You can see a person with your eyes, but can't see trust, honesty, patience, kindness, love, and hate. I can see all these things with my heart. I can sense when a person is friendly, kind, trustworthy, and loving. I have had some good days, sick days, lonely days, sleepless nights, but I'm not going to worry about anything! I have everything a human being needs to survive—shelter, water, food, air, nurture, and most of all, love.

We only have a few more days left on this Earth, so my Bible says! There are many people who can see, but they are blind when making spiritual decisions. My Bible also tells me that every eye shall see Him. I believe that with all my Heart. One day, we all will be able to see the whole picture. I can't see what you see, and you can't see what I see!"

"The Lord doesn't see things the way you see them. People judge by outward appearance, but the Lord

looks at the heart." (1 Samuel 16:7).

August 2019

Margaret couldn't get out of bed. Her body was weak. The doctor was called, and she had to go to the hospital. She could no longer stay in her beautiful apartment. It was time for others to make decisions for her.

Satan tried to make her think that it was all over. She had to get rid of the negative thoughts that were going through her mind. All through the day, she was thinking to herself, "I am well and able. I will do what I need to do. Nothing's too hard for my God. He will take care of me. I am strong in the Lord." She could hear her grandmother's voice saying to her, "Don't you worry, you just wait!"

...

Traborn Rehabilitation Center, Durham, North Carolina

The shuttle bus transported Margaret to Durham's Rehabilitation Center. The staff and employees welcomed Margaret to her new home away from home. They decorated her room with flowers and some of her favorite books. They provided a phone so she could call her friends and family. She had visitors every weekend. Everyone was friendly and offered to do what they could to make her comfortable. The first shift nurses made sure everything was ready when she arrived. Her meals, bath time, her medicine, her likes and dislikes. She didn't have to worry about anything. They treated her as though she had been there all the time. They were her new family and she loved them all.

Therapy would be a long and painful process. There were many stages to healing. But Margaret was a fighter and was ready to do whatever she had to do. Every day there were range of motion exercises, arm lifts, pedals, and ropes.

The work got harder each day, but she didn't give up. She knew that *"The Lord helps the fallen and lifts those bent beneath their loads." (Psalm 145:14).*

The time had come for Margaret to consider leaving the rehabilitation department. She was advised by her doctor to remain in the facility for more help. She could no longer live alone. Her health was declining to the point where she needed skilled nursing assistance.

So, during that same week, she was moved to her room. The assistants decorated her walls with pictures and placed flowers on her table. Everything that she needed was right at her hands. She was able to receive family and friends when time was permitted.

It didn't take long for Margaret to adjust to her new home. Breakfast was served every morning in her room, or she had a choice to go to the dining room. Lunch time was her favorite time to eat. The food was more like what she preferred during the middle of the day.

Dinner was a time to fellowship

with the other residents. She enjoyed meeting new people. Every holiday, the community would shower the residents and staff with gifts and fruit. As the days and months passed by, Margaret was content with her way of life. She had family who would call and talk to her for hours. Her sisters and brothers would call from New Jersey to see how she was doing.

Margaret made up in her mind that she wouldn't give up. She knew that God would take care of her. "I have no regrets," she said.

"We can rejoice, too, when we run into problems and trials, for we know that they help us develop endurance. And endurance develops strength of character, and character strengthens our confident hope of salvation. And this hope will not lead to disappointment. For we know how dearly God loves us, because He has given us the Holy Spirit to fill our hearts with His love." (Romans 5:3-5).

Chapter 11

• • •

2022

Three years have passed at the time of this book's publishing. Every day is a blessing to wake up and feel the blessings of God. If a person thinks about it, we are all living for the same tomorrow. Whether you're rich or poor, blind or can see, we all hope for the same things—having somewhere to live, being able to go to work; having food to eat; transportation to go and come; health, or if we are sick, having means to be taken care of, and most of all, being able to sleep—having peace of mind, and love!

Margaret is enjoying life now! She's going to do what Hattie asked her to do. "Don't you worry my child. You continue to put your trust in God. You're going to see His face some day. You were chosen by Him. Get up with God in the mornings and go to bed with Him in your heart at night. You wait on Him for the rest of your life."

"And then at last, the sign that the Son of Man is coming will appear in the Heavens, and there will be deep mourning among all the people of the Earth. And they will see the Son of Man coming on the clouds of Heaven with power and great glory. And He will send out His angels with the mighty blast of a trumpet, and they will gather His chosen ones from all over the World- from the farthest ends of the Earth and heaven." (Matthew 24:30-31).

Afterword

. . .

"I was born in 1949. I have lived over the age promised by God. I can truly say, He has been good to me. If someone would ask me if I have ever wished that I could see, my answer would be—that is wishing for something I totally don't know anything about! Who knows the troubles I would have encountered if I had my sight! God knew me before I was knitted in my mother's womb. He knew exactly what His plans were for me. I never doubted God! I never worried about not being able to see. I have always had someone to help me with whatever I needed. He provided for me. When I was sick, God was my healer, not man! I still depend on God for all my needs. He said it in His Word!"

"Don't worry about anything; instead, pray about everything. Tell God what you need and thank Him for all

He has done. Then you will experience God's peace, which exceeds anything we can understand. His peace will guard your hearts and minds as you live in Christ Jesus." (Philippians 4:6-7).

— *Margaret Marie Hailey Crudup*

About the Authors

. . .

Irene Hailey Harrington (left) and
Margaret Marie Hailey Crudup (right)

Margaret Marie Hailey Crudup was born on May 25,1949 in Wadesboro, N.C. to the late Effie Louise Hailey Watson and Edward Elliott. She is the granddaughter of the late Lexie and Hattie Mae Hailey. She was diagnosed with Congenital Glaucoma in the early months of her life.

She attended the North Carolina School of the Blind and Deaf in Raleigh, N.C. The name of the school was later changed to Governor Morehead School, from which she graduated in June 1968. She studied Sociology at Shaw University in Raleigh, N.C.

Later in life, she married Donnell Crudup, with whom she had three children—Demetric, Lamonte, and Sonja.

Margaret always encourages others to do their best, and to try to keep a positive attitude toward their goals in life. She is grateful for all the many blessings that God has bestowed upon her. "If I had to live life over again, I wouldn't trade it for anything that I have accomplished in my life. I would like to thank my family members and friends for all

their support, love and care they offered to me throughout my life thus far."

. . .

Irene Hailey Harringon is the
author of several books including A
Churchman's Confession, Coley Hill, A
Call Worth Answering, The Apple Tree,
and The Suitcase. A native of Wadesboro, N.C., she is one of ten children.
She and her husband, Maurice, are
the proud parents of three children.
  She credits her love of writing to
learning from her elders. She writes histor-
ical fiction to pass along this knowledge to
younger generations so it will never be lost.

Family Album

. . .

*Effie Louise Hailey Watson
(Margaret's Mother)*

Hattie Mae Hailey
(Margaret's Grandmother)

Lexie Hailey
(Margaret's Grandfather)

George Watson
(Margaret's Stepfather)